The File on
H.

The File on

H.

Ismail
KADARE

Translated from the French of

Jusuf Vrioni by David Bellos

 ARCADE PUBLISHING

NEW YORK

First published in Albanian under the title *Dosja H.* (1981)
Original title in French: *Le Dossier H.* (Fayard, 1989)
Translated from the revised version of the French text in Ismail Kadare,
Oeuvres, tome IV, Fayard 1996.

This is a work of fiction. Names, characters, places, and incidents are either the
products of the author's imagination or are used fictitiously.

Arcade Publishing books may be purchased in bulk at special discounts for
sales promotion, corporate gifts, fund-raising, or educational purposes. Special
editions can also be created to specifications. For details, contact the Special Sales
Department, Arcade Publishing, 307 West 36th Street, 11th Floor, New York, NY
10018 or arcade@skyhorsepublishing.com.

Arcade Publishing® is a registered trademark of Skyhorse Publishing, Inc.®, a
Delaware corporation.

Visit our website at www.arcadepub.com.

10 9 8 7 6 5 4 3 2 1

Library of Congress Cataloging-in-Publication Data is available on file.

ISBN: 978-1-61145-799-5

Printed in the United States of America

The File on

H.

1

THE DIPLOMATIC BAG from the Royal Albanian Legation in Washington, D.C., arrived on a gloomy winter's day, of the kind that nature bestows with particular prodigality on the capital cities of small and backward states. It contained visa applications from two Irishmen settled in New York, together with a covering note, which described the applicants first as "folklorists," then as "alleged folklorists." Everything else about them was rather sketchy. It seemed they knew a little Albanian, that they were intending to travel the country in search of ancient Albanian heroic songs, and that they would bring a quantity of filing cards and maps relating mainly to the Northern Zone, the area where they proposed to base themselves. In addition, and this was the most amazing thing, they would be bringing with them instruments that recorded voice and sound — weird, previously unheard-of contraptions that were called tape recorders and that, as the legation officials explained, had only just been invented and made available. The covering note concluded: "One cannot rule out the possibility that the two visitors are spies."

Two weeks after the arrival of the Washington bag,

and just a week before the Irishmen were due to land, the Minister of the Interior wrote to the governor of the city of N——, repeating more or less exactly what the legation staff had written to him, except that where the legation staff had said: "One cannot rule out the possibility that . . . ," he wrote: "Apparently these visitors are spies." All the same, the minister went on, the men should be observed with the greatest discretion so as not to alert them in the slightest, and generally speaking, the authorities of N—— were to behave in such a manner as to make the foreigners feel quite at home.

The minister smiled to himself as he thought of the surprise the governor would have on reading his last sentence. "You nincompoop!" he said to himself. "In your godforsaken hole, how could you understand anything about affairs of state?" The window of the minister's office allowed him to survey the roof of the Foreign Ministry. He was well aware that envoys from the neighboring ministry were scouring the capitals of Europe in search of some hack writer or pseudohistorian who might be commissioned to write a biography of the king. "Sure, sure," he was fond of repeating, "those guys at the Foreign Office are all properly educated types. So they get to do the glamorous jobs, like tracking down a biographer, but when there's business to be done, like picking up high-class tarts in Paris bars for the monarch, or finding a catamite for the Speaker, or sorting through all manner of sleazy business, then who do they turn to? Why, to me, the Minister of the Interior!" In spite of everything, he would end up scoring a point over those Foreign Office pansies. If it was he and not they who managed to turn up the king's prospective biographer, then that would shut them up once and for all! He thought of it every time there were foreigners in Albania, but no really promising opportunity had turned up so far. These Irish scholars, though, seemed just about made for the job, especially as they were suspected of being spies. He would leave them alone for a while to get on with their business, and then, with a bit of luck, he would catch them in flagrante (the phrase summoned up a mental picture of a conjugal bed in which one of the foreigners would be discovered in the very most rudimentary attire, in the company of a woman). Then it would be his turn to deal with them. "Come this way, my lambs. Let's forget about heroic songs, *tapregorders,* and such for a while, all right? Sit down, let's talk things over. You're going to do something for your friend. You don't want to? Well, upon my soul, you're going to force me to show you how angry your friend can get. Ah, I see you've decided to be reasonable. That's just fine! Now we're talking. What your friend needs won't be hard for you to do at all. You're scholars, aren't you? Your file says that you studied at Har . . . Har . . . Harvard. Yes? Excellent! Take a seat, please. Your friend will bring you paper and pencils, he'll get you candy, girls, whatever. But take care! You mustn't make him angry! You're going to write the life — the biography, as people say these days — of the monarch. That's what your friend needs you to do."

With a sense of satisfaction, the minister sealed the envelope addressed to the governor of N——, and then he hit the wax so hard that the seal jumped and made two imprints. The governor received the envelope two days later about ten in the morning and glanced at the seal for a second before breaking it. Experience had taught him that marks of that kind were only ever made by a hand moved by fear, or by anger.

When he read the note inside he felt relieved. "Nothing of the sort," he said to himself, then he lifted the receiver to give his wife the news.

The cloud of melancholy under which she picked up the telephone was condensed from dozens of disappointments when, having heard it ring, she had rushed to answer in hopes of receiving some uplifting news that would relieve the monotony of her life, only to be greeted through the perforated Bakelite by her husband's trivial interrogations — "What are you doing at the moment?" "Is lunch ready?" — or even by the postmaster's wife, with whom all possible subjects of gossip had long since been exhausted, asking some silly question about making jam.

This time it turned out to be quite different. What her husband had to say was truly unbelievable, to such a degree that in her astonishment, and fearing she had misheard, she said twice over out loud, "Two Irishmen, here? Is that what you said?"

"Yes, yes. They're even going to stay quite some time."

"How wonderful!" she said, unable to contain her glee. "What good news! I was feeling so low. . . ."

She had indeed spent an unutterably drab morning. The windows were streaked with rain, as they had been the day before. Seen through the dripping-wet panes, the chimneys on the other side of the street all looked

4

crooked. My God, another whole day just like yesterday, she had thought, sighing as she lay on her bed. Not a single idea managed to take shape in her mind: for the likeness of this day to the last seemed to her the clearest proof that it would be another quite useless day, a day she would gladly have done without. For a moment she thought that a day like this would be pointless for anyone on earth, then abruptly she changed her mind as she realized that thousands of women, after a hard week's work, or a family quarrel, or even after catching a cold, would envy her just for having the leisure to rest in comfort.

Such were her thoughts. Not many people would easily have accepted that, with all her material blessings, the attractive wife of the governor of N—— was miserable in that little town. But all of a sudden the telephone had rung, and the day, wound up like a string by that bell, had been transformed from a slack stretch of time into its opposite — a day full of surprise and mystery.

"Two Irishmen here for quite some time!" she muttered, repeating to herself her husband's words. "What a miracle! This winter will be different!" Her husband had given her to understand that he had received orders to make the foreigners feel completely at home. But of course, she thought as she pictured the cards laid out for bridge, the fire in the hearth, the glint of flames reflected in the crystal glasses. The governor had gone on to explain that the Irishmen were bringing strange contraptions, something like gramophones but much more modern, and she imagined herself in the arms of the one, then in the arms of the other, dancing the tango to the tune called "Jealousy." They must be pretty young to be lugging around all that gear.

She ran back to the phone, but as she picked up the receiver she froze. Before passing on such radiant news to the postmaster's wife, she felt the need to savor it all alone for a little while longer.

There are two of them, she thought, and most likely both of them are young men. Her husband had even told her their names: Max Ross and Bill Norton. He must also have been informed of their age. She would find a way of eliciting that information from him over lunch, without seeming to.

Moving automatically toward the bathroom, she stood for a moment in front of the cold and gleaming bathtub, then her hands reached out toward the hot-water tap. She began to undress with slow and sensual movements. She put two fingers into the water to test the temperature, then, when the tub was half full, decided to get in all at once. Quite often when her mind was occupied with thoughts of a particular kind she would soak in the bath and let her imagination wander.

As she lay stretched out with half-closed eyes, she watched the water rise and cover her body. That is how the dead are buried, she found herself thinking, but she cut off that thought, as she always did when a macabre or even just a painful idea came into her head. "No, no!" she said to herself. It was far too soon to indulge in such imaginings. She was still youthful; she was only thirty-two. Wasn't she awaiting a miraculous event, the arrival of those two foreigners? She said their names aloud to herself: "Max Ross. Bill Norton." They were proper European names. She had been quite right when, years before, she had changed her unattractively Oriental-sounding name, Mukadez, to Daisy. Most people had forgotten, and some were even unaware, that she had once had a different name; but when anyone who remembered used her old name, whether absent-mindedly or maliciously, she considered that person immediately as belonging to the enemy camp. Daisy was a name that sounded good. Who knows what those two would be feeling if they knew that a young woman called Daisy was thinking of them right now, in her bathtub? She often tried to imagine what people looked like from the sound of their names. And that is what she began to do with the foreigners.

Max Ross, she imagined, would have red hair and lots of it (perhaps because of the letters *x* and *r*, or even more because of the *s*'s), whereas the other one, Bill, she saw with hair smoothed down, a less virile figure, but no less dangerous. She had wanted for years to meet someone with just such a name, a fluid, slightly ambiguous name, all the more attractive for being hard to pin down.

The hot water covered her completely now, and she realized that she had forgotten to bring her bar of soap into the bath. No matter! She would just lie there and soak. Perhaps it would be even pleasanter without soap. She had noticed that in similar circumstances, lather disturbed both the clarity of the water and the flight of her fancies.

Through slanted eyes, she looked at her white body beneath the water, with the black triangle of her pubic hair refracted into a double image. In this shifting focus she found a kind of creeping dreaminess, which made everything vague and ambiguous. Though she tried not to admit it to herself, she knew that her boring provincial existence made her ripe for a sentimental adventure. It was no coincidence that a few minutes earlier, when the water was just reaching her waist, she had stopped herself from thinking the morbid thoughts that had tried to seize her. An emotion she had caught from watching romantic movies at the cinema stimulated her imagination and, so to speak, laid down a path for it. Images of that kind ran before her eyes and she found it increasingly difficult to suppress them. Chaotically, without attempting any logical sequence of thought, she saw herself first entangled with the hairy redhead, Max Ross, not because she was really attracted to him but by force of circumstance, or rather by the desire to encounter the whole range of initial sophisticated emotions (rivalry, exacerbated jealousy, etc.), before plunging fully into an affair with the other, Bill. "Oh my God!" she exclaimed suddenly and to herself, without ceasing to look at her water-enveloped body, as if it was the sight of her own nudity that had brought this thought to her mind. Just because her lover bore such a wonderful name would not prevent his making her pregnant!

She shifted awkwardly in her bath, like a sleeper turning over in bed. The gurgling of the water and the sight of the refracted curves of her body set her imagination wandering again. She saw herself, ashen-faced and visibly terrified, climbing the front steps of an ivy-covered two-story house. On the door was a brass plate bearing the name of the only doctor in N—— and, beneath it, the word *Gynecology.*

Tests Daisy's husband had agreed to have after years of dithering had proved that it was he who was responsible for their childlessness. Since then, Daisy could not imagine having an affair without an aftermath at the doctor's clinic to remove the traces.

So she would have to appear before the man who, in the gloomy cast of the town's characters, played, or seemed to play, the role of disillusioned doctor (for that is how provincial doctors are portrayed in films and in the stories of a Russian writer named Chekhov). "An accident?" he would ask, as his eyes traveled lasciviously over those parts of her body where not long before the drama of love had been played out but which were now as cold as the marble tiles of the consulting room. And she would then think: You flabby provincial quack! How can you understand anything at all about this tragic miracle?

She shifted once more, the water rippled for a few minutes and then calmed, and once again she could see the shape of her body in all its whiteness, anguish gone. Why did she allow herself these thoughts? Real joy, with its combination of pleasure, curiosity, and mystery, was just around the corner; she didn't need to make herself ill ahead of time with such mental contortions. A hand of bridge, a glass of wine, the warm glow of the hearth — these thoughts brought her back from her tragic tableau. All these things were almost palpably before her eyes and would be truly present within a few days. With a sudden burst of energy, she got out of the bath, put on a robe, and returned to her bedroom to dress.

Outside, as if nothing special had happened, it was still a soaking wet winter's day beneath a lead-gray sky, with drizzling rain tapping out the slow rhythm of life all around. Through the dripping rain the telephone wires would soon carry the news, first to the postmaster's wife, then to the other ladies of N——: something sensational was in the air.

Half an hour later, after making all her calls, Daisy went once again to the front window, which looked out over much of the little town. Though it looked quite unchanged, she knew that beneath that apathetic roofscape, her sharp-tipped news had hit targets all over the little town of N——.

2

DULL BAXHAJA, OTHERWISE KNOWN AS "THE EAVES," was the best informer on the books at N—— and had therefore been entrusted with the task of keeping an eye on the arrival and the subsequent words and deeds of the two foreigners. He wrote up his report for the governor on Saturday evening, that is to say on the day of their arrival. After standing about waiting for four hours at the travel agency opposite the bus station, on the lookout for suspicious characters waiting to rendezvous with the foreigners, he wrote, he had noticed nobody who tallied even remotely with such a target. In fact, his meticulous observation of the site had revealed that apart from the usual porters, there were in all nine people waiting for the bus from the capital, which came this far only once a week, namely on Saturdays, and that all nine had indeed greeted relatives immediately on their arrival via the aforementioned bus service, their shows of appropriate emotions demonstrating that their wait at the station had been fully justified. Save for the Gypsy Haxhi Gaba, of whom the governor had perhaps heard speak but whom the author of the present report failed to mention previously since it was a well-known fact that the aforementioned waited regularly for the Saturday

11

bus in the hope of finding among the travelers some person who might be inclined to slip him a few coins in return for his customary trick — "Your Honor will pardon me the expression" — namely the performance of an impressively long sequence of farts. As the honorable governor presumably knew, the above individual had been investigated several times for bringing the town into intolerable disrepute, etc., etc., but as far as the author of the present report was aware, the case had not yet received a satisfactory solution. In sum, apart from the doings of the aforementioned Gypsy, nothing suspicious had been uncovered by the investigator.

Although his particular branch was aural, Dull went on in his long-winded way, he had tried to accomplish his mission as scrupulously as possible, that is to say keeping watch on the foreigners from a distance, which in his humble opinion (if His Honor the governor would pardon such forthrightness) belonged more to the ocular branch.

So without claiming to offer advice to anyone, and certainly not to the governor, he would have thought that for this first phase of surveillance it would perhaps have been more sensible to employ the services of his colleague Pjetër Prenushi, an old hand at the oculars, whose abilities in this branch had long been unrivaled and had reached new heights on the day when — the honorable governor would perhaps recall — he had managed to spot from a distance of thirty meters that despite her exaggeratedly heavy makeup, the wife of the French consul, on a visit to their ancient city, was making eyes at someone.

Notwithstanding the aforesaid, and never wishing to question orders from above, he felt no awkwardness about taking on a task that was perhaps not strictly within his purview. On the contrary, deeply encouraged by the confidence that had been placed in him (even if it was perhaps on this occasion a confidence not entirely warranted on the part of His Honor the governor), he had as always spared no effort in fulfilling his mission as conscientiously as he could and in reporting the facts as laid out above with the greatest precision.

As for the two foreigners, it could not be asserted with absolute certainty that their behavior aroused no suspicion at all. In fact, it quickly became apparent that they were not at their ease, as evidenced by their constantly turning their heads this way and that, their weary faces, their hesitant gestures, almost certainly the symptoms of the anxiety, not to say the fear, that was torturing them.

They spoke first to Haxhi Gaba, in Albanian, making mistakes that were more likely the result of confused feelings than of genuine ignorance of the language. They took the Gypsy for a porter, whereas Haxhi Gaba thought he was being asked for his usual disgusting performance and was preparing to oblige, that is to say he was limbering up his whole body, so to speak, in order to expel the required quantity of air with sufficient force and sound — "I must ask Your Honor to pardon me once again" — so as to produce the sequence of farts that he imagined the two foreigners had ordered. The aforementioned was thus ready to perform his outrageous action — which he would have perpetrated this time, without a doubt, on what could indeed have been considered an international stage — when the present author, moved solely by a sense of patriotic duty and disregarding the fact that he was in no way authorized to do so, intervened and shooed the Gypsy away.

As for the suitcases and especially the metal trunks that the foreigners were lugging with them, the present informer had some difficulty in ascertaining anything about them on the basis of mere sight, especially as it was a well-known fact, as he had had cause to recall just a moment ago, that his field of action was essentially auditory, etc., etc.

On this point, while it was not his habit to meddle in other people's business, his sole concern being the smooth running of affairs of state, and while he would not wish to cast the eagle eye of his colleague Pjetër Prenushi in the slightest doubt, he felt obliged to point out that even Pjetër's gifts would hardly have sufficed to assess exactly the weight of the suitcases and especially of the metal trunks, let alone establish some relationship between the aforesaid weight and their contents. That said, he would take the liberty of suggesting that it might be appropriate to seek the opinion of the man who had hauled the load on his back, to wit, the porter Cute, also known as Blackie.

Blackie the porter: Suitcases? Don't talk to me about them suitcases, for God's sake, they nearly broke my back! Forty years I've been at this job, I never carried anything that heavy. Heavier than lead, I tell you! What

14

was inside them? Don't ask me — stones, iron, maybe the devil himself, but definitely not shirts and ties, I'll swear to it. Unless they were clothes of iron, like knights used to wear in the old days, the sort you see in the movies — but these were modern gentlemen, nothing to do with suits of armor, and they didn't look like madmen either. No, no, those weren't no ordinary suitcases of clothing. . . . Blackie can tell what's in a suitcase just by handling it. Soon as he hoists one up on his back, he can guess whether it's a rich man's, full of heavy, silver-embroidered cloth, or a padre's or a mufti's, with holy books inside, Bibles and Korans and the like. Nothing misses Blackie's eye where suitcases're concerned. He just has to stroke one to know if it's got a bride's clothes in it, all buoyed up with joy, or a widow's rags, weighed down with grief. Blackie's carried a heap of cases — the cases of happy folks, crazy folks, exiles running from the king's fury, desperate people expecting to hang themselves the next day with their luggage straps, the trunks of thieves, painters, women with their minds on only one thing (you can feel that right down your spine!), officials' traveling bags, hermits' packs, and even madmen's luggage half full of stones. Blackie has seen it all, he has, but those two, they had suitcases like Blackie has never carried in his life, for the love of God. They took my breath away. I thought I was going to split in two, and I said to myself, "Blackie, old man, you can say good-bye to this lousy job! Fall down and die rather than bear the shame of having to say: I can't carry that!" 'Cause Blackie once had a dream that was sadder than death. A traveler with a suitcase appeared on a road made of green and brown sticky cardboard and said, "Hey! Porter!" Blackie tried to lift the suitcase but didn't have the strength. There you are, it was just like in that dream — I was soaked in cold sweat under them damned cases. Those weren't suitcases but the devil himself!

The manager of the Globe Hotel: The suitcases were really heavy, but the trunks even more so. In order to get them upstairs to the room on the second floor — dear me! — I had to involve not just the usual bellboy but also two chambermaids and the cook.

The foreigners spoke to me in Albanian, but truth be told, the language they spoke was not our usual way of speaking at all. I don't know how to explain it, but it was like a tongue that was frozen in places, hard as ice, if you see what I mean. My job as a hotel manager involves meeting quite a few foreigners, so I'm used to all sorts of peculiar pronunciations. I don't mean to boast, but the truth is, because of these peculiarities I can tell straight off, without even looking at their papers, whether customers are Italian, or Greek, or Slav. Well, as for these two foreigners, it wasn't any of those kinds of accents. No, it was something completely different. Maybe I'm not making myself clear. They spoke a language that was . . . how shall I put it . . . like it had cooled down. A bit like the way my mother — may her soul rest in peace — came back to talk to me in a dream a few years ago. And I was so taken aback that I remember saying to her, "What have I done to you, Mother, to make you speak so?" Forgive my digressing like that, I beg you. . . .

Then what? Sorry, I almost lost the thread of my story! Well, they went up to the room we agreed to give them. Following your orders, we had sprayed it three times with insecticide, but dear me! I must confess I wasn't sure we'd managed to get rid of them all. They could have got in from the rooms next door, or under the doors, or especially they could have come down through the ceiling. But that's another story. . . . I just wanted to say that the foreigners stayed up there on their own until a messenger came from the governor, with an invitation to a game of bridge.

The governor's greeting, together with an invitation to drop in for a game of bridge, had been brought to the newly arrived travelers at around seven in the evening by the city surveyor. The surveyor's evidence, corroborated by the hotel manager (he had been up to knock on the door to announce that they were being asked for by an official gentleman), was that the travelers were rather surprised by the invitation: not only were they not expecting it but it had seemed so odd, not to say bewildering, to them that they took a little time to grasp what exactly was meant. The surveyor (like the hotel manager, of course) refrained from revealing, on reporting the foreigners' reply to the invitation, just how the governor's kind request had been greeted. But that did not prevent both of them from telling their friends that the travelers had hardly been eager, that they were fairly reserved, you could even say cold, and when they heard the word *bridge,* they seemed distinctly irritated. According to the city surveyor (and the hotel manager, of course) — this account had reached the governor's ears fairly quickly through the latter's own informers — the two travelers accepted the invitation more out of politeness than from any wish to play bridge. Oddly enough, far from being offended in the slightest by these comments, the governor mentioned this fact with evident satisfaction in his weekly report to the Minister of the Interior, stressing the degree to which the witnesses were honest and reliable folk.

All the same, the governor knew nothing of all that as he waited for the mysterious foreigners, together with his habitual playing partners — the postmaster, the magistrate, and Mr. Rrok, owner of the Venus soap factory, the only industrial plant in N——. But even if he had known, he would have said not a word of it to his friends, even less to their wives, and especially not to his own wife, Daisy, for whom the travelers' arrival was the most joyous event of the season.

Wearing a gently rustling sky-blue voile dress, Daisy, perhaps because of the rouge she had put on her cheeks or because of the dark circles under her eyes, seemed far away, as if she were slightly drunk. She went back and forth between the lounge and the room where the bridge table was set up, catching fragments of conversations that seemed to her ever more horrendously banal. They were speaking of the travelers who were due to arrive at any moment, speculating as to why they had chosen to settle in this town in particular. Daisy found such considerations quite scandalous. The very idea that they might not have come to N——, but could have gone to some other place seemed to her so horrible that the merest mention of that possibility, the miracle having happened, could put the whole thing in jeopardy, and she almost came to the point of fearing that the visitors might ask themselves all of a sudden, "Well, really, why did we pick N——? Isn't there another town where we could go just as easily?"

"That's what is really extraordinary," said Mr. Rrok. "Yes, it is really strange that they decided to settle here. You have to admit this is a godforsaken hole, off any road to other countries. It's not a historic site or a strategic town, as people say. A place with no name for anything in particular. And, what's more, stuck fast against the foot of the mountains."

"It seems they had set their eye on this area even before they left America," the postmaster asserted. "People say that as soon as they got off the boat at Durres, they hauled a map out of their bag and said, 'That's where we want to go.' "

As they chatted, they glanced now and then at the governor, but with a slightly weary smile on his lips (good God, how do you manage to keep the same smile on your face for hours at a stretch, for dozens of people?), with his early-evening smile on his face, he pretended not to hear them. In fact, he too had been wondering what made the foreigners choose the area of N—— for their puzzling business. On several occasions he had had an intuition that it would give him a lot of trouble; at other times he felt the opposite, that it could be advantageous to him. When he was feeling low he sometimes imagined that someone who wished him no good had packed these undesirable Irishmen off to him as part of a murky plot. All the same, though they might be wily foxes, they would this very night, the first night of their stay, reveal at least a part of what they were up to. In the confidential letter that he had sent to the minister by return mail on receipt of the latter's note, he confirmed it to be his view too that it was of the utmost importance to bring the travelers' secrets into the light. Yes indeed, the governor sighed, the state is deeper than the deepest well. While he was still wondering when the whole affair would become clear, the doorbell rang. The sound of the bell affected all present like an electric charge. Most of them turned toward him as if waiting for instructions on what to do, others put down their glasses of port on a table or on the marble mantelpiece. All except Daisy became feverishly agitated; she stood stock still, her eyes riveted on the landing.

Meanwhile the maid had opened the door, and everyone could hear first of all the sound of their steps on the stairs — a sound that the governor likened in his mind to the noise of wooden legs (maybe because he had skimmed through the reports that alluded among other things to the *stiffness* of the foreigners' Albanian, or maybe because it really did sound like that). In a flash, he caught sight of his wife's profile, which manifested her anxiety. Her hair was done up in a chignon, but a few stray blond wisps emphasized the grace of her smooth-skinned neck. With surprise rather than contentment, the governor wondered why he was incapable of feeling any jealousy on her account.

Without even bothering to hide her feelings, Daisy

kept her eyes on the two guests as they climbed the wooden staircase behind the servant girl, half turned toward them, who led the way. They did not look anything like what she had imagined. Neither of them had hair that was remotely dark, or soft, or flattened. Nor was either of them redheaded or hairy, as Max Ross had been in her mind; quite the opposite, one turned out to have thinning, fairish hair. As for the other, he had a strong and energetic face and somewhat darker but still unremarkable hair, which was moreover cut short like a boxer's. That could not be Bill, but on the other hand, with his affable appearance as of a tame hedgehog, he could not be Max either! She almost released a loud sigh: They were completely unlike what she had imagined, but fortunately, thank goodness, they were young men.

Her turn came to shake hands, and to her great astonishment, the blue-eyed one with blond hair, as he took her hand in his, gave out in antiquated Albanian:

"Fair lady, to thee I bow, thy servant Bill Norton. . . ."

"Daisy," she replied.

The visions that had come over her in her bath a few days before, her speculation about it all ending up at the gynecologist's, dozens of equally insane details, flooded back to her mind and made her blush.

So that's the one called Bill, she thought after a moment, as they completed the round of introductions. She had certainly expected them to be different, but she could not say that she was disappointed. That would not have been fair, especially when she imagined the possibilities for scientists — venerable duffers in slippers and ridiculous nightcaps readying themselves for bed. For the time being, what remained from all that was a sense of losing her balance. . . . She should have shown herself equally attentive to the other one, Max Ross, but though he had brown hair and his companion was blond, she felt herself inclining toward the latter, the one called Bill. It certainly was not his name but something else about him that decided her. Maybe a kind of gentleness, though very reserved and as it were constrained, together with his way of speaking, which seemed made of stone and which cast a cold shadow all around it. Daisy could not bear to be disappointed. Anyway, each is as handsome as the other, she thought by way of consoling herself, and what's more, both are young, even younger than she had expected. As for language, quite apart from speaking Albanian after a fashion, they both seemed to be in perfect command of English. *Darling . . . My dear . . .*

She felt suddenly that if she should have a sleepless night, her insomnia would be caused not by her being attracted to one or the other of them, as she had hoped, or by bitter disillusionment, but by something else, by the effort she was making to come to terms with the real appearance of the two visitors. During the night, and maybe for many more nights, she would suffer the changes that were needed to make her just as receptive to the reality of the Irishmen as she had been to her imagination of them.

Meanwhile the introductions were over, and the two foreigners felt that momentary awkwardness of blundering into a social gathering that had been in progress for some time. They smiled again at everyone, then once more at various individuals, until the governor, seeking to put everyone at ease, asked:

"Would you care for anything to drink, gentlemen?"

The thought of drinks and prospect of the visitors' choices relaxed the company somewhat. Everyone expected the foreigners to be connoisseurs of fine wines. Oddly enough, they were not. Perhaps this was what prompted the regulars to notice that the guests' attire was also quite surprising. It was, so to speak, rather casual, to put it mildly. All of which contributed to loosening the governor's tongue:

"I learned of your arrival in our fair city and I thought, They are far from their families, in a foreign land, in the back of beyond, and quite alone. That's right? So then I thought you might like to come to play bridge, that way you would feel less cut off. . . ."

The governor spoke slowly and articulated his words so as to be understood, and the foreigners nodded their heads.

"We thank thee, good sir," said the one with the crew-cut hair. "Albanians are for hospitality renowned."

"Do you expect to stay for a while?" Mr. Rrok inquired.

The foreigners shrugged their shoulders.

"Methinks a goodly length of time."

"We are delighted," the governor replied.

"Thank you, good sir."

Daisy thought that she recognized something familiar about their intonation . . . classes on ancient

Albanian versification at the girls' school. But she found it hard to concentrate.

"From what I have heard about you, you intend to study our folklore?" said the governor.

One of the visitors raised his eyebrows as if to delay replying, while the governor exchanged a rapid glance with the magistrate, the only person with whom he had shared his suspicions.

"How can I put it? Verily, indeed . . . and perchance other matters too," came the reply, from the one called Bill Norton.

"I'm sorry, but I did not quite understand."

The other foreigner furrowed his brow once again. "We purport to have much ado with your ancient song," he explained. "And perchance . . ."

"'Dawn came up from the couch of her reclining . . . ,'" Daisy recited to herself, the opening line of one of the epic poems in all the anthologies. That was the rhythm she could hear in the speech of the two visitors.

". . . and perchance with something most closely allied to it," the fair one went on. "We mean to say: Homer."

"Your good health!" said the postmaster's wife, as she raised her glass of port.

Despite her powdered face, she was visibly impatient to have these boring questions and answers come to an end and to learn more interesting things from the foreigners. Daisy had mentioned something about their having brought with them the very latest in gramophones. So what were people dancing to these days over there, from New York to California?

"You mentioned Homer?" the governor continued. "As far as I recall, a blind old Greek poet?"

"Why, yes!" Bill exclaimed in English, to Daisy's great joy. She turned triumphantly to the other women in the room, as if to say: Now you can see that they're real foreigners, speaking in English like that!

"Really, Homer? For three hundred years there has been some debate about whether there was one or several Homers. . . ."

Mr. Rrok, the factory owner, straightened his bow tie, spread a smile across his face from ear to ear, and shyly intervened:

"Pardon me, gentlemen. Out here in the back of beyond, we do not have much by way of scholarship. Myself, for instance, as I told you a few moments ago, I deal with soap — Venus soap, toilet soap for ladies. . . . Ha ha, that sort of thing I have at my fingertips. But as for deep questions of philosophy, Homer, Verdi, or what have you, I haven't got a clue. So please excuse my ignorance, but tell me: what connection can there be between Homer and your esteemed journey to Albania? If I am not mistaken, Homer lived four or five thousand years ago and quite a long way away from here, didn't he?"

The postmaster's wife could not restrain herself from a loud sigh of exasperation. Daisy had always told her that Mr. Rrok had no more brains than his bars of soap had legs.

The foreigners exchanged smiles that the governor judged to be full of meaning.

"Verily, about three thousand years ago, good sir," one of them said. "And far away from this place. But the connection exists nonetheless."

The shadowy smiles that the governor had thought full of meaning returned to their faces. Hmm, now they're making fun of us openly, he thought. They're definitely trying to pull our legs. How could one believe that they were really looking for a solution to the mystery of Homer in a small town that had never had any connection whatsoever with the poet? Couldn't they have found a more plausible excuse for coming? But even on that score they didn't seem to have made much of an effort. Provincials, they must have thought, peasants living in a backwater. . . . Ha! We shall see who has the last laugh! You two may have seen all sorts of things, the governor continued to himself while maintaining his unwavering smile, you may have looked at skyscrapers and things of that kind, but what you've never met before is Dull Baxhaja. When he gets on your tail he'll stick there like a leech, no matter where you are — on top of a skyscraper or in the ninth circle of hell!

The thought of Dull calmed him down for a moment. Then his mind went back to the note from the Minister of the Interior, or rather to the phrase about their being "caught in flagrante," after which, the minister said, "your mission will be terminated, the remainder being my concern." To tell the truth, the governor had no clear idea of what would constitute being "caught in flagrante." On this point the minister's epistle seemed to have been written hurriedly, even impatiently: he had gone so far as to give the bizarre advice to treat the foreigners well "even after they've been nabbed." "Treat them as before, but get them to understand that they've been caught in the act and that there's no point trying to get off the hook."

Now that he thought about it, the minister's letter seemed even odder than it had at first sight. It all might have seemed part of a game, if the minister hadn't repeated how important the whole matter was, much more important that a provincial official could imagine.

Taking pains not to be noticed, the governor looked at his watch. At the present moment, Pjetër Prenushi should surely have managed to open the suitcases and to photograph the piles of notes and documents that the customs report said they contained. And then, following the orders he had been given, he would have what looked like the most interesting texts translated, so as to get them on his boss's desk by dawn.

Feeling content, the governor was able now to smile without effort at everyone, including those who in his view did not deserve his attention. Pjetër Prenushi would definitely be running over to the ridiculous shack above whose front door a signboard announced in blue hand lettering, *Photo Lux,* while the owner of the premises, bent double by his painful piles, would be waiting inside in a state of terror. He would stop trembling only when he saw that he had to deal with texts written in English. Shots of corpses, of stolen bracelets, and especially of naked women, gave him the shakes.

The governor was now visibly at ease. The thought

27

of his two best sleuths in action outside in the dark, the cold, and the wet gave him special satisfaction. Others, he knew, were jealous of the perfect duo that afforded him his "ears" and his "eyes," but as for himself, he had a distinct preference for Dull. And whenever rivalry between them was at issue, either because of some spat or on a question of pay, though he always tried to appear fair, he generally took Dull's side.

We are not a very developed country, he liked to philosophize from time to time, and as in any country of this kind, the eye does not play a preponderant role as far as intelligence is concerned. Most people here are illiterate, and even those who do know how to read and write do not like to do so often. Very few write their memoirs, keep a diary, or have a regular correspondence. Even wills, which are hard to imagine as not written down, signed, and sealed, are still frequently oral. And do you know what stands in lieu of initials and the duty stamp? Curses! "May you never know a single day of happiness in this world or the next if you do not carry out my wish!" "May you turn into a tree!" "May the earth never accept your corpse!" And so on and so forth.

That is what he liked to say on the matter of eyes, but as soon as ears were the issue, he changed his tone completely. Ah, ears, gentlemen, are a quite different matter! The ear never rests, for people always want to talk and to whisper; what is said and especially what is muttered is always, as you all know, much more dangerous to the state than what can be seen. At least, in our country, he would add. And if the governor was among a group of very close or very reliable friends, he would indulge in recalling his one and only real failure in intelligence matters. A failure due, of course, to the "eye": in letters from a provincial Don Juan to a Tirana tart called Lulu (the correspondence was naturally checked because of the king's open flirtation with the aforementioned tart), he had read the words *organization* and *secret* ("I swear it, those really were the words that I thought I deciphered, hidden like two hares in a thicket made of allusions to Lulu's belly, to her delta, to her thighs!"), whereas what was actually written was *orgasm* and *secretions*! Good God, he still blushed as red as a beet whenever that misadventure came to mind. . . .

Mr. Rrok's conversation with the guests was still in progress, and the governor took a few moments to pick up the thread.

"Verily, there is a true and real connection, good sir," the fair one was saying, "but it grows late, and there is not time to give the reason tonight."

"Some other time, without fail," the other one said, in an odd kind of lilt. "Weary we be, for our voyage was long. . . ."

"But of course," the governor said to himself. "It's time you worked out your cover stories! You didn't even bother to do it in advance. Ah, my unhappy province, to be so despised by mere spies!"

Someone suggested a hand of bridge, but the foreigners shook their heads. They repeated their litany about the tiredness caused by such a long journey; but the biggest surprise of all was that they did not know how to play! That was just too much!

Once the idea of bridge had been abandoned, the ladies took charge of the conversation. By far the most talkative among them was the postmaster's wife, beneath the half-patronizing, half-ironical gaze of Mrs. Rrok, the soap manufacturer's spouse.

"I am deeply shocked to see how our own dear friends can hardly wait to meet the foreigners, so as to put on airs and graces and lead the young men on," Mrs. Rrok whispered to Daisy, who turned away abruptly toward the fireplace, so as to hide her blushes. After busying herself for a moment at the hearth, she could turn back to Mrs. Rrok and show entirely justified bright-red cheeks. "I find this thirst for adventure quite revolting!"

Daisy smiled absentmindedly. She realized that Mrs. Rrok was irritated at not being able to show off her knowledge of Italian, but that at least allowed the magistrate's indolent wife to feel smugly satisfied. It was she who asked the visitors:

"Will you be settling in at the Globe Hotel?"

"Nay, ma'am," they replied together, almost as one.

The magistrate smiled sourly.

"So where else do you expect to stay? The Globe is the only decent hotel in our town."

"Nary in town," said Bill. "We shall go hence."

"What?" Daisy cried out, as if something had burst inside her heart. She had avoided looking into the eyes of her guests, as one puts off one of life's enhancements until later, but now she turned a wild stare straight at the man who had chilled her heart by uttering such an ice-cold sentence. Daisy's glance was at once heated, reproachful, and enticing, a combination that ought to have led the man to change his mind, but the foreigner only repeated his merciless words.

The governor had moved away from his guests momentarily, but now he came back to lend an ear to what was being said about the newcomers' accommodation. And what he heard was really odd. The foreigners were explaining quite openly that notwithstanding the pleasure of present company, they had no intention of hanging about in the town. No, they weren't off to any other town, certainly not to any other area; they were going to stay in this zone, for sure, but not in the town of N——, and anyway, they wanted to have as little as possible to do with towns. They would lodge in a wayside inn far from any other houses, a remote hostelry or, more exactly, one of those coach houses located where major routes intersect. If the cold weather had not already come on, they would have gone up into the highlands to carry out their research, but as the hills were now deep in snow, they would have to settle for a lodging at the foot, beside the old highway, as they said, one of the places where traveling singers usually put up. In fact, they had already pinpointed the inn they had in mind, and it was not very far away.

"Ah! You mean the Cross Inn," the soapmaker butted in. "It's beside the main road, about halfway between Shkodër and Tirana."

"Nay, sir," replied Max Ross. "'Tis called the Inn of the Bone of the Buffalo, or, for short, Buffalo Inn."

"Oh," said the postmaster, "but that's a very old inn, and so far away from anything that even telegrams take four days to get there."

The Irishmen let out a gentle laugh.

"We saw it on the chart," said Bill. "It is the place that best befits our task."

"Obviously!" the governor muttered to himself. "You couldn't imagine a better place for your secret machinations!"

"So you have also brought maps along with you?" he inquired aloud.

"Aye, a goodly number. And all the epic areas are marked."

Wonderful, thought the governor. They are not even bothering to pretend anymore. He was tempted to ask them what these epic areas were but chose instead to pretend not to have noticed the term.

"Where is this Buffalo Inn, then?" Daisy asked the postmaster's wife in a whisper.

"How can I explain? I don't remember very well. I only went there once, with Petro, but it's such a tumbledown place it makes you shiver just to see it — it looks like a heap of ruins."

"Unless I am mistaken," the governor interjected, "it is, with the exception of the Inn of the Two Roberts, in central Albania, the oldest house of its kind and has been in existence since the Middle Ages."

"And is it very far from here?"

"No, not really. An hour's drive in a cart, I guess."

Daisy felt warmer. An hour in a horse-drawn carriage wasn't the end of the world.

The conversation around the foreigners had got livelier.

"You really are amazing," Mr. Rrok was saying, with his face right up to theirs, smiling under their noses. "Myself, for instance, I deal in soap, and I reckon I understand a bit about the world insofar as . . . well, we all have something to do with soap, don't we, all day long, from dawn to dusk. So, as a result, when I think about it, I say to myself, Soap is important, universal, and it seems everybody else thinks that way too. Because in fact you know it's not a joke, it's something that has to do with the body. There's soap for shampoo, there's toilet soap that does its job well or not so well, aside from all questions of scent, not to mention any other qualities or defects, for instance excessive acidity, which can be harmful, as you may well understand, to the delicate skins of ladies, especially when they wash their private . . . Ha! So anyway, I can have the illusion that everyone thinks of soap just like I do. But then along come two gentlemen like you, who are not in the least interested in my bars of soap and who have got it into their heads to come all the way to the end of the world to stay in a pigsty of an inn and try to find out about a blind guy who lived a million years ago! What a funny world this is!"

"What a dismal idiot," the governor said to himself. The revenue inspector had not been wrong a couple of years ago when, over some card-game squabble, he had told Mr. Rrok to go jump into his own vat and turn himself into a bar of soap.

With the help of her maid, Daisy served coffee. As

the governor sipped from his cup, his mind wandered to the hotel manager, who would by now have had ample time to sift through the entire contents of the travelers' suitcases.

The foreigners' faces were now showing signs of real weariness. And the evanescence of the face powder of the postmaster's wife was an unmistakable sign, well known in the tiny social world of N——, that midnight was nigh. Despite everyone's efforts at stifling their yawns, sleep hovered in the air.

A lull in the conversation gave the foreigners an opportunity to make their farewells. They stood up and bowed and, on the landing, were asked by those showing them out whether they remembered the way back to their hotel or if they would like an escort. Then Mr. Rrok declared that he would like to walk them back himself, which aroused both general approval and a degree of regret, though at this late hour of the night no one could rightly say what the grounds of the regret were, or if indeed they had any relevance to soap.

Shortly after, the other guests took their leave, and the house soon resounded only to the couple's own footsteps. In the tense silence of the night, the sound seemed to take the two away from each other, though they must have ended up in the bedroom together. As she undressed before joining her husband in bed, Daisy tried her best to put the two foreigners (or, more exactly, one of them) out of her mind, but once the bedroom had become totally dark and silent and the faint squares of the windowpanes could be made out opposite the marital bed, at long last, as if she had found the path on which to direct her thoughts, she turned them with complete naturalness toward the man she had just met, just as she used to do when she was a girl. What could he be doing at that moment?

The two Irishmen got back to their hotel a little before midnight, Dull Baxhaja wrote in his report. As per instructions, he had gone up into the attic, and well before they got back from the party, in fact at ten-thirty precisely, he had taken his position over the room where the foreigners were staying. After checking the state of the ceiling (the gaps between the boards would permit him not only to hear whatever might be said but also to see a bit), after checking also what kind of creaking would occur if and when he was obliged to move one or another of his limbs, and, furthermore, after ascertaining the risk of falling through a rotten plank (even now, after so many years, he still felt horror at the memory of the night when his right leg had suddenly gone through the ceiling of the Shkjezis' bedroom, sticking down like a surrealist lamp fixture and giving the old lady the heart attack that took her to an early grave) — after having taken all precautions, then, and despite the fact that the rafters were crawling with bugs and other repulsive creatures, he applied the rules recently issued by counterespionage personnel management (rules intended in the first place to minimize drowsiness and above all actual sleep among on-duty surveillance operatives) and took out his little tin of personal bugs and spread them about his person.

As mentioned at the head of the present report, Dull Baxhaja continued, the two foreigners had returned to their room a little before midnight, and they had begun to pace back and forth, from corridor to bathroom door, as if worried about something. From time to time they exchanged a few words in their own language, which made no sense at all to the present observer, and that was not because some of the words were uttered by one or the other of the suspects while brushing his teeth: as the governor would know, the present observer was able to distinguish words pronounced by individuals having not just a toothbrush but any manner of object in their mouths, be it a pipe, a cigar, or, as in the case of Maria K., who habitually put it there during lovemaking (the governor will pardon the following), an organ that cannot possibly be named in the context of the present report. The present writer was thus perfectly able not only to grasp all such speech but also to understand a suspect who spoke while chewing, or with a sore throat, or with three-quarters of his teeth missing, and in many analogous circumstances, to such a degree that — as the governor must have been informed — Dull Baxhaja, "The Eaves," was the one and only spy in the whole Northern Zone of the kingdom capable of interpreting the speech of a man struck down with apoplexy. No, to repeat, if he had been unable to understand the dialogue between the two suspects, it was not because they were brushing their teeth most of the time (a dialogue, and a brushing, that went on for some considerable length of time), but for the simple and obvious reason that the conversation took place in English, an idiom that, as the governor must surely be aware, the sleuth Dull Baxhaja did not understand.

After brushing their teeth, the two foreigners opened their suitcases, took out their pajamas, and went to bed. It must be emphasized that they exchanged yet more words in the dark before going to sleep. Nothing to report for the rest of the night. Nobody knocked at the door; our two customers therefore did not open it; nor did either of them go to the window, so no signal was given by lantern, by lighter, or by any other means. The only detail perhaps worth recording: one of them went to sleep, as the observer realized straightaway, but the other stayed awake, tossed and turned in bed, sighing heavily and scratching himself. With the exception of the last detail, whose cause was easily guessed (though the hotel manager had sworn thrice over that there were no bedbugs here), it was hard to understand why one of the miscreants should have sunk into slumber while the other stayed awake, and even harder to grasp the reasons for the contortions and sighs of the latter. The sleuth would like simply to observe that his long experience had taught him that in similar cases — in other words, where the miscreants are two in number — it is not unusual for fear, doubt, anxiety, indeed even thoughts of betrayal, to prevent one of the partners in crime from sleeping in peace. So that was perhaps the reason for the difference in behavior between the two in the present case also. But there could of course have been other reasons: for example, one of them may have had a guilty conscience, and as everyone knows, that can disturb one's sleep, whereas the other, the less dishonest of the pair, could sleep like a log; unless it was the other way around — that the really crooked one, hardened to this kind of adventure despite his tarnished conscience, was sleeping soundly, while the one who was but a beginner in the trade and had not yet been blooded was unable to quell his inner torments. These finer points perhaps went beyond the sleuth's mission, and the governor may well have formed the view that his agent was treading on ground well outside his areas of competence for the pettiest of motives, such as ambition, a desire for promotion, or just vainglory. But he wanted it understood that no such assumption would be justified, and that if he expanded on such and such topic or came close to appearing impertinent by dealing with matters that were not strictly his concern, then he did so not for any of the base motives mentioned but because he was convinced that he was thereby doing his job more satisfactorily, for when all is said and done, did the governor himself not declare, at that meeting he held with us all, that spies were not merely listening instruments but living beings, servants of the state enjoying not only the right but even the *duty* to interpret what they had been asked to do in as creative a manner as possible?

To come back to the reasons for the sleep of the one and the sleeplessness of the other suspect, the sleuth added, the reasons could be quite different from those suggested above. He was close to concluding simply that the two fellows had maybe arranged to parcel out roles, one sleeping while the other kept watch, for security reasons.

The spy also mentioned which bed each of them was sleeping in and added a sketch of the scene to his report, so that with the help of the hotel manager, it was easy to ascertain which of the two researchers did not get a wink of sleep.

3

THE ONE WHO COULD NOT SLEEP was Bill Norton. Although usually a light sleeper, he had thought that with the fatigue of the journey, the late night, and especially the few glasses he had drunk at the governor's party, he would nod right off. But that did not happen. An hour after getting into bed, he realized that he was going to have a sleepless night. A flea or bug bite had sufficed to shatter the fragile, unconscious partition between sleep and waking. The hotelier's words "I can assure you there are no bedbugs here; only yesterday I sprayed your room with insecticide," together with the smell of disinfectant and the memory of the dreadful bus ride and their arrival at N——, the search for a porter, all coming on top of their reception on entering Albania, in that filthy customs office, and then the ogling of the governor's wife, especially as he'd thought such transparent banter had had its day long ago, and finally the hotelier's assurance, ". . . unless of course they come down through the rafters": all these superimposed impressions overlaid, so to speak, by an inexplicable anxiety, the kind of alarm one feels when it seems that someone is trying to force open the front door of one's

40

house — all that had him tossing and turning in bed all night long.

Two hundred yards away, the sole photographer in the town of N——, who with Pjetër Prenushi's help had reproduced every page of the newcomers' notebooks a couple of hours before, was now developing the film beneath the spy's baleful stare. Pjetër was still smarting from the slight inflicted on him by the governor when he awarded the initial surveillance of the foreigners to Dull Baxhaja. "So do you believe me now, you numskull?" he muttered angrily to himself. "Thought you could do without me, didn't you? But you've seen the light at last, haven't you, that we're dealing with educated folk, the type of customer that doesn't just say what's in his head without thinking but puts it down in writing. OK?"

The prints, still wet, were laid out to dry, and the photographer was fishing the last ones out of the sink. Ha! Dull could train his ears as long as he liked, but what these foreigners had in their heads was right there in black and white!

Pjetër Prenushi lit cigarette after cigarette as the photographer, his face drawn and haggard from lack of sleep and ill health, took the very last prints out of the developer.

The agent looked at his watch from time to time and snarled, "Come on! Come on!" just to keep the old man on his toes.

It was two o'clock on the dot when Pjetër Prenushi's cart rumbled under the windows of the hotel where Bill Norton was still tossing sleeplessly in his bed. Pjetër was on his way to Zef Angjelini, the friar, the only man in N—— who could translate English into plain Albanian.

At precisely two-thirty, Brother Zef, after crossing himself and praying that God forgive him "yet another sin," began to work on the translation.

"Oh my God," Bill groaned, burying his head in the pillow. It wasn't his first sleepless night, far from it, but it was unlike any other he had known. He felt ever more stressed, and the luminous hands of his watch, which he glanced at every so often, made him shiver as if they glowed with a deathly light.

The cart rumbled under his window once again at six-thirty. Bill was now quite exhausted, emptied of all his reserves.

"Good grief, here they are!" mumbled the governor, still half asleep, as he heard the horse-drawn cart trundle up to his door.

He slipped out of bed very carefully, so as not to wake his wife and went downstairs.

Pjetër Prenushi, resentment written all over his face, handed him a large envelope.

"Well done lad," the governor said, without even looking at the agent. "Off to bed now."

The governor went back up to his study and took out the sheets of translation, together with a short covering note: "Herewith the documents you requested urgently. P. P."

The governor let out a heartfelt sigh. Ah, it was nothing like Dull's report writing! Nothing gave the governor as much pleasure as those reports, not even — though he would have been ashamed to admit it — not even romantic novels.

"At last!" he thought as he unfolded the sheets covered with the priest's beautiful handwriting. "Now let's see what those nuts have in their heads," he added, feeling a twinge in his heart. The pain accompanied a vague feeling of guilt at receiving reports from someone other than Dull Baxhaja.

"At last!" he said a second time, as he settled down to read.

After a while, the governor raised his head and rubbed his eyes. He had never liked books, but unlike the other officials at N——, he did sometimes read. Gossips said that it was only because of his wife, but he didn't mind. During their long, boring evenings together, overcast by that marital tension which is far more treacherous than an outright row, what he'd do to clear the atmosphere was not to whisper soothing words to Daisy, or to promise her an outing to Tirana, or to smack her around, as other husbands did, but simply to pick up the book that had been lying for ages on her bedside table and open it. He would then feel his wife's eyes on him, attentive at first, then sympathetic, as if she felt sorry to see him mortifying himself on her account. Thereafter her to-ings and fro-ings between bedroom and bath would accelerate, the rustling of silk would become more audible, until the awaited moment when she would tiptoe up to him and place a kiss on his forehead. Those were the sweetest moments they had, especially when with her dainty hand Daisy closed his book and took the spectacles off his brow.

Reading had thus been long associated in his mind and in his senses with the smell of powder, so that in the absence of this stimulus, it seemed doubly tiresome to him.

However, there was another reason why, on this occasion, reading seemed unbearable. He had been waiting to see these pages with impatience, almost with anxiety, and they disappointed him. They were opaque, incomprehensible, and — this was the main thing — profoundly suspect.

They consisted mostly of notes written in diary form, with a few short letters interspersed. They dealt with learning Albanian and shorthand. Frequently, also, they mentioned keeping things secret. Now and again there was a note of disquiet. "We must hurry, or it will be too late."

Why did they have to hurry? For what might they be too late?

The governor skipped through to the end of the manuscript in the hope of finding further oracular phrases, but there were very few of them, and they were always buried inside stodgy paragraphs that seemed to have been designed to hide them.

So that's that, he sighed, when he realized that whether he liked it or not, he was going to have to work through the whole text if he wanted to glean any inkling of the plot. It had been written by Bill Norton.

I remember that boring afternoon when I slouched on the sofa, not knowing what to do, and switched on the radio. It seems so far away, like in another world. The program I tuned in to was just as boring — Professor Stewart, giving the old routine on Homer, the dispute that's been going on for three hundred years, with version A versus version B, and version C to cap it all — oh boy, was that dreary! Was Homer really the author of the Iliad *and the* Odyssey, *or was he just some sort of redactor, or more precisely the chairman of a committee set up to write it all down . . . ? "Of course, if we prefer to use contemporary language . . . ," and right on cue, the interviewer chuckled to keep the professor company. Boring! I was going to get up to turn the volume down, I even thought, That's a program that might just impress a team of accountants, when, at that very moment, the classicist answered one of the interviewer's questions with a digression. A blessed digression that stayed my dial-turning hand: "Is it silly to wonder if there's a country or region in the world today where such epic poetry is maybe still being invented?" "Well, no, your question is not silly at all," Professor Stewart replied. "Quite the contrary, it is a very interesting question. . . ." And to my amazement (if not the amazement of accountants), the classicist explained that such an area did indeed exist, that it was not a very large area, and it was the only one in the world where that kind of poetry was still cultivated. He said exactly where it was: in the Balkan peninsula. More precisely, it covered the whole northern zone of Albania but extended also into parts of Montenegro and reached a few parts of Bosnia, inside the Yugoslav border. The radio professor explained: "This region is the only place in the world where poetic material of the Homeric kind is still being produced. In other words, I would say that it is the last surviving foundry, the last available laboratory, if I may use a modern expression, which can still bring back . . ."*

The governor nodded. So let's see what comes next, he thought.

The following pages described how this broadcast had amazed Bill Norton. This was where the two fools first expressed their fear of arriving "too late."

Small wonder that someone like me, a mere post-doc from Ireland who came to New York with my friend Max Ross in the (far from certain!) hope of adding something new to the old debate about Homer, was dumbfounded. The last available laboratory, I kept saying over to myself. The last surviving foundry. I was rather disoriented and kept mulling the words over as if my intellect refused to take in their meaning. On the radio, the voice droned on, but I wasn't listening anymore. "The last available laboratory in the world," I said aloud at last, as if that would shake my brain out of its daze. Very soon that foundry would disappear. It was already threatened. It had to be made use of before it was too late. Before it fell into ruin, before it was buried under the sands of time, before it was forgotten.

I was startled to realize that I was pacing up and down the room. I would have preferred to think of the whole business in a state of calm, but that was out of the question. Good God, we must hurry! I thought. We must get over there as quick as we can. Discover that ancient laboratory. That thousand-year-old foundry of verse. Study it close up, as through a microscope; listen, as if we had stethoscopes, to the way in which Homeric matter, the Homeric marrow, is produced, and with that under our belts, it would be no trouble at all to unravel the mystery of Homer himself.

But shh! I warned myself. Not a word to anyone. Except Max Ross . . .

"The only area . . . ," I kept on saying to myself. The only area still able to give birth to epic poetry. The rest of the planet had passed through menopause. The only fecund region

*was there. The only place that was still hot.
The only place that could still be made pregnant with the very latest epic. If we waited
any more, it would be too late for anything.
Sand and forgetting would cover it all over,
all of it, even the puzzle itself. . . .*

"We'd already caught on to that," the governor said
to himself as he scrabbled for a cigarette with a hand that
shook from excitement. "Yes, we'd already caught on,
you old crook!" he said aloud.

He needed a few minutes to be able to concentrate
on reading again. As was to be expected, one of the pi-
geons had let on to the other, and both of them were now
overcome by their "discovery."

*. . . We were both high on thoughts of all
that was going to happen. It would shake the
world! They would beg us to accept a chair
at MIT! Definitive papers at the World Congress of Mediterranean Archaeology! And in
our old Irish hometown people would shake
their heads in disbelief. Bill Norton and Max
Ross? You must have got the names wrong.
It must be some other pair. . . .*

*We laughed and laughed. And then we
started imagining all the consequences again.
Sing, O muse, of Harvard's anger! And of
the International Center for Homeric Re-*

*search! "And of my stupid mother-in-law,
Diana Stratford," Max added. . . .*

*But we had done enough laughing. We had
to leave at once for those distant parts, had
to get there, to the area, to the expiring laboratory. Issue a press release right away? No,
quite the opposite: keep it all very, very secret.
Pretend the idea had never occurred to us. All
that remained was to get started, there and
then. Without telling anyone what we were
up to.*

*We went over our good resolutions again
and again, and then Max looked hard at
me and said quietly, after a pause: "It is a
good idea, undoubtedly, but in any event,
you can't do anything without proper preparation. . . ."*

*Those were the first cold drops to fall on
the heat of our enthusiasm.*

"We'd already caught on to that one as well," the
governor mumbled as he stubbed out his cigarette in the
ashtray. "OK, let's see where the fox goes to ground. . . ."

He was convinced that the plot was right there but a
little more effort was needed to coax it out into the light.

*. . . Who was Homer? A blind poet, as mil-
lions of educated folk imagine, or a redactor,
or even, as Stewart claims, an editor in chief?
The ancient poems of the* Iliad *and the*

Odyssey edited and published by Sir J. F. Homer, of the Grecian Academy — ha ha ha!

Meanwhile our minds were racing toward the Balkan peninsula. According to Stewart, there were rhapsodes still living there. Certainly the very last of the rhapsodes, the last Homeric singers. We would listen to their ballads and record them. That much was clear. But we wouldn't just record different singers; we would compare them each to each. That was also common sense: confronting different rhapsodes and comparing the different versions. But would that be enough? We entered the two types of work into our notebooks, and as we did so we realized that the adventure that lay ahead would be much more complex than we had thought at first.

The governor reread the paragraphs he had just deciphered: proper preparation . . . comparing the different versions . . . adventure that lay ahead . . .

OK, let's see where you go to get your instructions, he thought. Your university — or some office of the Greek intelligence service?

Once again, he was disappointed. The glimmer of light that had begun to clarify his suspicions was replaced by a thick fog of boring prose.

We finally laid our hands on a recent and very complete edition of Albanian epic poetry.

With the names of the itinerant singers whose ballads were reproduced. We could publish a collection of the songs of other rhapsodes. That way epic poetry would have a thousand faces. Like the reincarnation of a single being by metempsychosis.

We are less interested in Albanian epics themselves than in their production process, to use a modern term. We are seeking to reach by induction a truth of universal applicability: the means by which epic poetry is generated, and as a consequence, the answer to the enigma of Homer.

The comparative method is the main key to our work. Not just comparisons between the different rhapsodes. The most important comparison will be the different interpretations of the same song by the same rhapsode. In other words, his way of singing such and such a poem one day compared to the way he sings it some later day. A month later, say, or three months later.

Apparently the issue is not just a question of memorization. It is also related to a fundamental aspect of oral poetry — the mechanisms of forgetting, which in its turn is not really just a matter of forgetfulness but a much more complicated business. There could be involuntary loss of memory, but at the same time, conscious memory loss is

*involved. An alleged slip of memory justify-
ing a new interpretation of the song . . .*

The rhapsode is the main wheel in the machinery of the epic. He is publisher, book-
seller, and librarian in one, and also rather
more than that: he is a posthumous co-author
and, in this capacity, has the right to amend
his text. It's perfectly legal, no one disputes
his right, and no one criticizes him, except
perhaps his own conscience.

It now seems obvious that the question
which formerly seemed fundamental for
explaining the Homeric phenomenon — to
wit, how many lines could a rhapsode commit to memory (some say six thousand,
others eight thousand, or even as many as
twelve thousand) — needs to be replaced
with a different question: How many lines
may a rhapsode wish to forget? Or rather:
Can a rhapsode exist without a capacity to
forget?

We must stress, in this connection, that
we still know very little about the world of
the rhapsodes. What sort of people are they?
How is their gift acquired? When is their art
recognized publicly? On what does their rep-
utation rest? What causes them to return to
ordinary life? How are the contests between
them held? What are the different styles, or
schools, or rivalries between them within this

*strange universe of recitation? How are the
mediocre performers filtered or weeded out?
How are criteria of value established?*

*We'll try to find out all that when we are
there. With a bit of luck, we will manage to
enter this universe, and then we shall understand how the yeast was made to rise in the
ancient dough. As it always has done. As it
did in H's time.*

Just as the governor was about to yawn, he lighted
on a passage that had what seemed to him to be a rather
literary touch:

*For the second time this week, I've had a bit
of trouble with my eyes. The first time, it was
like a cloud in front of me. I thought it must
be from too much reading and took no notice.
Today it happened again, but it was slightly
different. It was as if I was looking through
a broken windowpane that would not stop
wobbling. It felt as though the vibration was
damaging my retina. After which my sight
stayed misty for quite a while.*

I must go and see an optician.

As always in such circumstances, the governor had
the impression that he could smell his wife's powder. He
could see it sprinkled on her smooth belly, just where the

pubic hair began, but carnal desire, instead of slowing down his breathing, as it usually did, filled his eyes with cruelty.

To ward off any evil imaginings, he struggled to focus his mind again on his utterly boring reading.

There are three hypotheses put forward by German scholars, who were the first to study the common motifs in the Greek and Albanian traditions, the migration of material from one mythology to another, its splicing, transferal, and cross-fertilization. The first view is that the process of the creation of epic poetry has come to an end in Albania. The second view is that the process is still alive. And the third view is a compromise: even if the age of the Albanian epic is effectively over, the embers are still hot and could throw out some last bright sparks. The same scholar takes the view that even though the production of new epics is dying out, the foundry itself, however derelict it may have become, is still actually there.

So we must hurry. Make haste before the embers go cold! Before the foundry collapses!

"Before the embers go cold . . . ," the governor repeated to himself. In his mind, which had been shaped by detective mysteries, "embers" summoned up images of *sleepers*, agents who had been put in place long ago, then of a nunnery, then of an old conspiracy, then, suddenly changing direction, it took his mind back to his wife's sexual organ.

"Stop that now!" he exclaimed, and put his head down into the papers again. He would force himself to read them, even if they were in hieroglyphics!

How does living material, or, more prosaically, inanimate raw material, how does material in general enter the epic machinery that turns it into art?

That is another chapter, just as fascinating as the question of forgetting.

The Germans claim firmly that you can still find Albanian rhapsodes who convert contemporary events into epic poetry (who can Homerize modern life). It would be really extraordinarily good fortune to see such a miracle happening before our eyes.

Every time the question of this transformation arises, I think back to an old, long-abandoned tannery on the outskirts of Dublin, not far from where I lived. That's how I imagine the ancient Homeric workshop.

When an event goes through those old rollers, belts, and vats of dark and sinister liquid, what happens to it? How do the rhapsodes' lungs, brains, fantasies, passions, and even their heredity contribute to the process?

*It is all rather like an embalming process.
Yet it's not a corpse that is being treated, but a
piece of life, an event, most often an unhappy
one.*

*At bottom, epic poetry itself, seen as a
whole, is no more than a kind of morgue. It's
no coincidence if the climate of the epic is
always cold, indeed colder than cold. The
temperature is always below zero. Moreover,
there is a formulaic phrase that comes back
time and again, like a refrain:* This sun shines
brightly but gives little warmth. . . .

The governor reread the preceding passage and then
underlined the words in the middle of the page, *dark and
sinister liquid,* trying all the while to keep his mind off
Daisy's body. But he couldn't, because the notes became,
once again, just like a novel. . . .

*I can't get to sleep. The lights of the city twinkle
through the windowpanes. As they go out
one by one, I feel as if I'm floating in the
Milky Way.*

*There are billboards out there, one adver-
tising ketchup and another vitamins that are
good for the eyes. My optician prescribed that
for me.*

*I imagine our two names, Bill Norton and
Max Ross, alongside Homer's (good God,
like two assistants helping a blind man across*

the street!) in newspaper headlines and on the illuminated news display.

"Yes, go blind, then, the two of you, blinder than your hero!" the governor exclaimed, and enjoyed the relief that he always felt when he uttered a curse. "Well now . . . ," he said a few seconds later, as he came across the words *happy day.* "Let's see what made our two dickey birds so happy."

Oh, happy day! Day of surprises. And of luck.

I could easily believe in divine intervention. Can't be a coincidence that the magical elements magnês *and* phônê, *which make up the original word for the machine, seem to come from ancient times.*

What has brought magic to this day, and to our forthcoming pilgrimage, and to our whole enterprise, is the word made up from magnetic *and* sound, *the magnetophone, or, as the manufacturers call it for simplicity's sake, the* tape recorder.

It is a machine that records the human voice. That you can take with you, wherever you go. That not only records but plays back, as often as you want. . . . It's exactly what we need! Like a gift from the heavens! Sent to us by providence! From Olympus!

Hmm . . . The governor stifled a cough. So that's all their machine could do. . . . He had been imagining all sorts of things: a cinema camera, an oilfield detector, a bomb intended to blow up Parliament . . .

Careful now! he warned himself as his eyes fell on the name of the king:

We are also learning more and more about Albania. A small country with an ancient population. Tragic history. To begin with, a European country. Then Asian overlords. Return to Europe in the twentieth century. Half of all Albanians live outside the current borders.

Apart from the epic, which constitutes its principal treasure, in our view, Albania also has chrome and oil. And a king, Zog, whose name means "bird." King Bird the First . . .

I had another appointment with the optician. Got a fresh prescription.

Max is having problems with his wife.

We're trying to get the money together so as to buy the tape recorder as soon as possible.

We are revising all our ideas in the light of the machine. Oddly enough, bringing a tape recorder into our work is no trouble at all. The device fits our project so well that it seems as if we had designed it all from the start with the machine in mind. As if, sub-

consciously, it had preexisted its own invention . . .

The governor skipped through several more unutterably boring sheets. His eyelids were drooping, but he sat up with a start when he came across the words *minister* and *spy.*

"You're getting closer and closer, my friends," he mumbled as he reached for his cigarettes. "You're walking right into the noose."

As he read on, he said those words to himself over and over, but without really knowing whether the *noose* was the Albanian Legation in Washington, or Albania itself.

We just got back from Washington, where we submitted our applications for Albanian visas. I can't hide the fact that we were rather disappointed by the way the Albanian Legation treated us. Not at all warm. On the contrary, the atmosphere was all suspicion and mistrust.

The plenipotentiary, who saw us in person, took our breath away. The representative of this partly archaic and partly grotesque little monarchy turned out to be intelligent, crafty, and witty, to have an extraordinary knowledge of world literature, to speak all the main European languages (including Swedish). He was even the friend and patron of the French poet Apollinaire, and he pokes fun at everything, most especially at his own country and its people. Although we were trying to be as vague as possible about the reasons for our visit, we couldn't help mentioning the name of Homer — and the diplomat interjected:

"Did you know that some people claim that in the first line of the Iliad, *'Mênin aeidé, thea, Pêlêiadéô Achilêos' ('Sing, goddess, of the anger of Achilles, son of Peleus'), the word* mênin, *as you can see for yourselves, is the Albanian word* meni, *meaning 'resentment'? Which means that of the first three or four words of world literature, the first and unfortunately the bitterest is in Albanian. . . . Ha ha!"*

Then he went on talking about Albania with such cutting irony that in the end Max said to him:

"Your Excellency, I find it hard to know when you are speaking seriously and when you are joking. For instance, what you said about the word meni, *which you find in Homer — is that a learned jest or is it . . . ?"*

The diplomat's eyes flashed with a fearsome mixture of intelligence, cynicism, bitterness, and malice.

"As far as the word is concerned, I believe that what I told you is in effect correct, and yet . . ."

He fell silent and his face darkened, with only a twinkle of humor left in the corner of his eye, while his pupils shone with a fierce glow. After the words "and yet," there was a long pause, which became ever more menacing, so that for the second time, unable to bear this lapse in conversation, Max interrupted:

"And yet, Your Excellency?"

"And yet" — the diplomat came to the point at last — "the Albanians of today maybe have nothing at all in common with the way you imagine them."

"We don't imagine anything at all," I answered. "So far, you are the first Albanian we have ever met, and I can't hide the fact that we are, well, overwhelmed."

The diplomat began to laugh again, while the consul, who had been present throughout without saying a word, stared at us with an obviously suspicious eye. When he glanced sideways at the maps that Max had taken out of his briefcase to show the plenipotentiary, I suddenly thought: Good God, of course — the consul takes us for spies!

"The consul assumed we were secret agents," I said to Max as we walked away from the legation. "I realized that too," he replied. "But what do you think of the plenipotentiary?"

> *"Amazing!"*
>
> *"Amazing?" said Max. "That's an understatement. . . ."*

The notes ended there. The governor rubbed his eyes. Funny business, he thought. His mind felt a complete blank.

Something attracted his attention to the window. It was the rain that the wind knocked against the pane from time to time. Dawn had risen on one of those really filthy days that give you somber thoughts, like a debt to settle next week or the fear of having a cancer you've not yet mentioned to anyone.

"'The consul assumed we were secret agents,' I said to Max. . . ." The governor read these words over and over, shaking his head. "What crooks!" he mumbled. "They think they can cover their tracks by planting words like *agent* and *spy*! Like pyromaniacs who give the first alert! What they're trying to say is, As we are as white as the driven snow, we are not afraid to say the word *spy*. . . . But they can't pull the wool over my eyes! They must really be spies, and maybe far worse. All this nonsense about Homer and the rhapsodes is only camouflage, hiding their true, murky mission. They wrote those notes up on purpose and left them on purpose in their suitcases, so that even a dolt like Pjetër Prenushi would have no difficulty getting hold of them.

"You cretin!" the governor said aloud to himself, bursting with anger. "You utter idiot! You gave me the envelope, proud as Punch, as if to say, See what *I* can do! Ah, you poor misguided fool! They ran rings around you, they took you for a ride, you blockhead! But it won't work with me. Oh no. I can see that all these scribbles are just eyewash. Let's wait and see what Dull has to tell us...."

As usual, the thought of Dull calmed the governor's nerves. It was not for nothing that he liked to say Dull was his balm, the secret of his restful nights. Every time he felt a sudden anxiety, the kind of anxiety that is all the more troublesome for being without obvious cause, he would think of Dull squeezed into some chimney or squatting on some blackened beam, and his nerves would be calmed down. He is listening, the governor would think; he is tracking down evil....

"Whereas you, Pjetër, birdbrain that you are, you've swallowed it hook, line, and sinker!" The governor roared out loud. "They shoved a load of paperwork under your nose, and you said, Thank you, that'll do nicely! Filthy spies!... Bastards!...."

The governor was overcome with waves of anger, rising from his gut. He thought he could hear the shutters banging again, but it was the door, which had just opened. Startled, he saw that Daisy had come in.

Still warm from bed, wearing only her transparent nightdress, Daisy had crept up to him on tiptoe. Good God, what softness she exudes! He was right to tell her that she was much prettier half asleep than in any of her fancy outfits....

"What are you doing?" she whispered.

He covered up the documents with an almost automatic movement of his hand, even though her sight was still too clouded with sleep for her to make out any words.

"As you can see, I'm working . . ."

"You gave me a fright. Has anything happened?"

He stroked her hair. "Go back to bed. It's still very early in the morning."

The wind rustled and hissed outside. The governor watched his wife's hips swing provocatively as she left the room, but his eyes glowed with an icy stare.

Somewhere in those papers there was an allusion to fecundity, or fecundation, something about getting on with it before it was too late. . . . There was even something about Homeric seed!

He riffled through the papers in a frenzy. Ah, there it was. He had remembered correctly, except that the word used wasn't *seed,* it was *marrow.* But didn't that come to the same thing, really?

Then he understood the real cause of his muffled fury. Every time he heard mention of sterility or fertility, he felt as if allusions were being made to his wife. Or even worse: he imagined that whoever used such words desired Daisy and was yearning to pour his own sperm into her. To make her with child . . . before it was too late . . . before menopause set in . . . before dusk.

Hadn't one of those foreigners made eyes at her during the soiree? It was plain as a pikestaff, he realized, plain as a pikestaff. He was quite prepared to believe that they had come from the other end of the earth for the sole purpose of sleeping with his wife.

Curiously, the governor's jealousy was tinged with

a strange kind of desire, which welled up so strongly that he nearly fainted from it.

The distant bell of the Franciscans' chapel spread its gloomy resonance over the rain-sodden town, as if to insist on its own repentance for some past failure. He imagined Brother Zef celebrating the morning service with eyes all red and swollen from a sleepless night; perhaps the image of one of the nuns had crossed his mind briefly. That would account for his having translating the Irishmen's passionate language with such ardor.

The governor's thoughts returned to Daisy's alabaster body, which doubtless made him an object of envy. Surely people dreamed of possessing his wife and making her pregnant. . . .

He was disturbed by a feeling, different from his usual desires, that ran through him from head to toe. Getting up from his desk, he went noiselessly into the bedroom and gazed at Daisy. She appeared to be sleeping peacefully again, and despite her seeming more desirable than ever, he did not dare wake her.

Daisy was not sleeping. When she heard the door creak on its hinges, she shut her eyes and slowed her breathing. She must have had an erotic dream in the first light of morning; she still felt limp.

A gloomy day had dawned outside. Even the chapel bells sounded as if they were in pain.

She wanted to cross herself, but she was quite numb in the bed's warmth and had lost all wish to execute the slightest physical movement. Instead of making the sign of the cross, her hand glided lazily over her breast and then her belly. She was on the brink of tears.

Bill, three hundred yards away, did cross himself. He was only half awake, but even though he barely heard the church bells, his hand moved automatically to his forehead, his chest, each shoulder. . . .

It had been a truly hellish night for him. Only in the small hours had the anxiety that had racked every part of his brain finally subsided and given him some peace. In the faint light of dawn, he could make out the dull gray mass of the metal case containing the recording machine. Hi there, buddy, he thought, with a feeling of calm and joy. He liked the peace that the day's dawning brought him. Even the bugs seemed to be drowsing; they were certainly less ferocious now.

Bells are rung differently here, he managed to think just before he dropped off again. But the lonesome and lugubrious chimes, such as he had never heard anywhere else in the world, continued to reach his ears even while he slept.

4

A SMALL CROWD WAS WAITING on the pavement to watch the two Irishmen emerge from the Globe Hotel, or rather to get a glimpse of their luggage. Blackie the porter had sworn by all the gods that there was sure to be some nasty surprise when the cases were loaded. Maybe the hotel staff who had been given the job (Blackie had waited in vain for the manager to hire him) would stumble under the weight, maybe they would fall, maybe they would even break their backs. He hinted that the carriage could easily veer off and end up in the ditch. Apart from the terrible weight of those accursed trunks, there was that peculiar sensation the porter had felt in his head between the bus station and the hotel, which — he was sure of it now — came from the foreigners' cases. Well, then, he surmised, if a human brain could be affected like that, just think what might happen to horses' heads. Without his actually saying so out loud, it was obvious that Blackie reckoned the nags might very well bolt and hurtle the carriage, the driver, and his passengers into a ravine.

Lym the coachman had heard the gossip, but he turned up nonetheless at the appointed hour at the steps of the Globe Hotel, demonstrating that he was prepared to test the porter's sinister prophecies. The word was that when he had been told of the porter's assessment of the relative mental strengths of man and his main helpmeet, he had retorted that his horses were at least brighter than Blackie. All the same, when the foreigners appeared at the hotel doorway, the onlookers, who had been there for several hours waiting to see how the whole business would end, definitely noticed an expression of worry on the face of the coachman and in the trembling of his horsewhip.

Large raindrops were falling irregularly. However, the two travelers would not get inside the coach until they had seen their luggage properly stowed. The hotel staff, including the porter and even the manager himself, who had tried to lend a hand, had wobbled now and again as they brought the luggage out, had even nearly stumbled, but none of them actually fell. (They'll collapse on top of each other like dominoes, I swear by Allah they will, Blackie had promised; they'll fall on each other like pieces of meat on a shishkebab, then they'll scatter like chickpeas.) On the other hand, something happened that neither Blackie nor anyone else had foreseen. One of the travelers looked up at the sky anxiously, whispered something to the other foreigner, then both seemed to be about to make some point to the hotel boy who was carrying one of the trunks, then the first foreigner slipped off his raincoat and put it over the trunk, while the other nodded in approval.

"Ah, I see, they seem to want to protect that trunk from the rain. It must be full of . . . full of . . ."

"Full of what?" a voice asked.

No answer.

"What do you think could be in it?" the voice insisted.

The first speaker stared at his questioner with wide eyes. "If you're that eager to know, why don't you ask them yourself?"

The second speaker just shrugged his shoulders.

Meanwhile the coach had set off, and the onlookers' necks all turned in the same direction, as if connected by an invisible string.

Within fifteen minutes the coach had left the little town and was rolling along an empty country road. Max and Bill looked out of the tiny openings in the side doors, onto the desolate plain, which looked even wilder at its edges.

Bill rubbed his eyes with the palms of his hands.

"Is there fog on the plain, or am I just seeing things?" he asked.

"It really is foggy," said Max.

Bill sighed with relief. I must stop worrying about that, he thought. Ever since they had left the town, it had seemed as if his sight was veiled once again by a wispy shroud. But the shroud was covering the plain, not his retina. It cheered him up, and he began to whistle.

"Beautiful, isn't it?" he said after a while. "It feels as if today is the real beginning of our adventure."

Max nodded gaily.

Above the half-dismantled and rain-sodden haystacks, black birds were wheeling, their wings seeming weighed down by the enormous raindrops.

"The farther away the inn is from here, the better for us," Bill said. "We'll be able to get on with the work in peace. Otherwise we'll have half our time taken up by small-town society calls."

"I bet they'll come out all this way to get hold of us."

"You think so? Then we'll just have to be absolute bores."

"Easy to say," Max replied. "But I think we have to do the opposite and be extremely accommodating. They could give us a load of trouble."

"Maybe if we told them more about the work we're planning to do, they'd leave us in peace," said Bill. "After all, it's in their national interest."

"Do you think they give a damn?"

"How should I know? Maybe you're right. Looking at a country from afar, you imagine that every inhabitant is eager to slave away for it, but when you get nearer . . . Actually, I guess it's the same with us. Hey, look, more haystacks. . . ."

"I've never seen such haystacks — they look like ragged beggars," said Max.

"Maybe because they've been in use. It *is* the end of winter. . . . What were we saying?"

"About local society . . ."

"Oh, right! If we get involved with those people, that's the end of our work. I think I even heard them talking about a ball. . . ."

"Really?"

Max burst out laughing. They joked about being invited to a provincial ball, then Max teased his friend about the governor's wife.

"I thought I saw her making eyes at you."

"You think so?" Bill rocked with laughter.

"Buffalo Inn . . . Buffalo Inn," Bill chanted, to the rhythm of the carriage's creaking wheels. A proper medieval name for an inn. The longer the journey continued, the safer they felt from the dangers of bridge games and dances. The ruts and potholes on the road, which bounced the carriage about, offered supplementary protection against provincial cardplayers.

The inn stood by the roadside. Even before the carriage had come to a halt, they noticed the roof of flat stones, then a blackish balcony with a wooden balustrade, and finally the main door, which the wind blew back and forth on its hinges.

A tall boy with a jutting chin and wet, chilblained hands hobbled out on wooden clogs, whose clacking made it seem that he was moving faster than he really was.

Then a man came out to greet them. "I am the innkeeper," he said. "My name is Shtjefen. And this is my lad, Martin," he added, pointing to the boy. "I am happy for my inn to house such unusual guests."

His eyes looked sincerely glad, even if his mustache drooped at the tips as if mortified by some unknown offense.

"'Inn of the Bone of the Buffalo,'" Bill spelled out from the sheet-metal sign nailed onto one of the swinging doors. "That's a very old name, isn't it?"

"Indeed it is," the innkeeper replied. "It's been handed down from generation to generation. They say it's been in existence for nearly a thousand years."

Max whistled in admiration and cast his eyes over the soot-blackened beams above their heads.

They ascended the dangerously creaking wooden staircase in single file. The innkeeper pushed open the door to one of only two upstairs rooms.

"Here is your room, gentlemen. The bedsheets are clean. If you wish, you may make a fire in the fireplace. At night the wind blows a lot, but if you close the shutters you won't hear or feel a thing. They're thick, made of oak, and bulletproof. And here are some slow-burning candles for the night."

The innkeeper's eyes lit up, and then he furrowed his brow in thought.

"It's very odd, but two weeks ago I dreamed that I had two guests who were very different from my usual clientele. They came on horseback, and their mounts had, in place of manes, unlit lanterns hanging around their necks. . . . I thought in my dream: Let's hope that is a good omen! And then, two days later, news of your visit reaches me. . . ."

The foreigners exchanged glances.

"Does it happen that rhapsodes sometimes lodge at your inn?" Bill asked.

"Rhapsodes? Hmm . . . Of course they do. Even though . . ."

"Yes?"

The innkeeper made a wide gesture with his arms, as if to express deep regret.

"They used to come much more often. These days there are not all that many of them left."

"How come? That's not what some people reported

to us. Apparently your inn is at the point where all their routes cross."

"That is right, sir. And I am glad that you know. It is perfectly accurate information. Perhaps I said more than I meant. What I meant to say was that in the old days there were more players of the *lahuta,* the long-necked instrument with one string, with which you may be familiar."

"That goes without saying," both travelers said simultaneously.

"So . . . But if you want to see these singers," the innkeeper continued, "then there's nowhere apart from here that you'll find them, except perhaps at the Inn of the Two Roberts, where *lahuta* players still drop in, but that's a long way away."

"We'll talk again about that," said Max. "We really do want to get in touch with them."

"I'll be glad to help, gentlemen," the innkeeper said, as he stood to one side to let in the lads who were bringing up the luggage.

Late that evening, the governor was busy at his desk, drafting a report for the Minister of the Interior, and he glanced from time to time at the account that his informer Dull had written on the two foreigners' first day at the Buffalo Inn.

He does write well, the old devil, thought the governor. He may be a mere informer, but his prose is better than what you find in the *Albanian Effort.*

He had long secretly envied Dull's style, especially turns of phrase like "leaving aside the fact that this task is not incumbent upon the present writer," or all those "notwithstanding"s that he sprinkled around his sentences with such elegance. The governor himself used to try inserting the latter word wherever he could in his letters, even when it did not really fit, and on rereading his texts, he always found himself obliged to cross it out.

"Barely had they arrived at the Buffalo Inn and after exchanging a few words with the innkeeper (leaving aside the fact that this task is not incumbent upon the present writer, I am obliged to point out that some of the innkeeper's words, specifically when he told the newcomers that he had seen them in a dream, appeared to the present writer to be not only meaningless but quite inappropriate in the mouth of a citizen of our kingdom when speaking to foreigners) — after exchanging a few words, then, the foreigners remained in their room."

The governor skimmed through the report and stopped at the point where Dull Baxhaja described the opening of the suitcases and especially of the trunks that contained the machinery, not to mention the thousands of file cards that the Irishmen took out of various card boxes with great care. Actually, the spy went on to say, the visitors did not seem particularly concerned about hiding the cards; quite the opposite, in fact, since they used thumbtacks to fix some of the cards and especially maps to the walls, to the extent that within fifteen minutes there was not a bare space on any of the partitions or even on the inside of the door.

The governor skipped the pages where the informer described in every detail the testing of the tape recorder, the sound of which he was hearing for the first time in his life. According to Dull, the Irishmen had recorded their own voices, though the playback had a different tone from that of a natural human voice. This difference notwithstanding, Dull continued, he was able, by dint of his vast experience, to satisfy himself that it was indeed the foreigners' own voices, since the distortion made by the machine was identical to the alteration of a voice overheard from behind sheet metal, down a chimney, or through a decrepit wall.

What a sleuth! thought the governor.

He decided that the passage in Dull's report about the maps pinned to the wall was the part most worth mentioning in his own report to the minister. "The present author," Dull had written, "after having fulfilled the duties required of him in his posting under the eaves, managed to get a clearer view, from several angles, of the maps and of the markings made on them."

The governor reread several times the passage describing the maps. According to Dull, they looked like weather maps, such as he had seen on the only occasion that he had been to Tirana airport, when he was entrusted, as the governor will perhaps recall, with the surveillance of Mme. Maria M——, traveling to Malta and suspected of taking with her two ancient icons from the great church of Shkodër as well as a secret missive from Monsignor S——.

"There's really nothing this lad doesn't know," the governor said to himself with something approaching admiration. "Nothing escapes him; he only has to see something once, or, even more, to hear something, and he's got it. If he lived a hundred years, two hundred years, Dull would still have it all stored up in his memory. He is more precious than a great library, than the National Archives or the British Museum, and all other such things. "

According to Dull's thorough description, the maps were marked with a host of arrows, some of them circled, some curved, some straight, similar to the signs that indicate rain and wind in meteorology. Above or below the arrows were letters, or numbers, or both: A, CRB, A4, etc. On some of the maps, roads were marked by unbroken lines, as were the built-up areas alongside them. Even the Yugoslav border was marked on two maps.

Hmm. That's serious, the governor thought. These customers could not even be bothered to camouflage their game. Either they still think we are fools, or else . . . or else there's something even more important underneath.

Dull went on to give even more interesting clues. According to the spy, some of the maps were marked with large circles labeled "epic zone A" or simply "epic zone" or "authentic epic zone"; there were even areas labeled "epic subzone" and "semi-epic zone. "

It was all extraordinarily precise. The governor would have liked to copy this part of the report word for word, but he was reluctant to do so. It was not just a matter of pride — after all, nobody would ever know that he, the all-powerful governor of the town of N——, had plagiarized the report of a mere informer — but something of much greater weight: he was afraid of making a blunder. All these facts were laid out in the open, as if they were being displayed precisely in order to be seen. What if that was merely a trick designed to divert suspicion?

"Hmm . . . ," he said aloud. For a moment he was quite still, hesitant, his pen in his hand. He would do well to cast his report to the minister in such a way as to protect himself, however things turned out, against accusations of gullibility, on the one hand, and, on the other, of having been overeager to suspect the foreigners at any cost.

He started scribbling again, and as he added fine-sounding words to his unpolished sentences, he felt once again a pang in his heart. He was jealous of Dull. The more he thought about it, the angrier he became with himself. He tried three times to get "notwithstanding" into his report, but however hard he tried, he could not manage to insert it in the right place; it stuck out from the other words like a foreign body, like an unacceptable and even comical intrusion, and he crossed it out three times with a stroke of the pen that was more like the lash of a whip. "Oh, oh," he groaned aloud, "a vulgar little spy who can write better than I can! Well, anyway," he added by way of self-consolation, "flowers grow better on dunghills."

After much effort, he finally managed to deliver himself of a paragraph in which he informed the minister that in view of the maps and the arrows marked on them, and notwithstanding the foreigners' professed interest in the movements of rhapsodes across northern Albania, there was every reason to suspect them of being involved in intelligence activities. It was still unclear how they intended to use the rhapsodes to transmit or receive information or coded messages. For the time being, and as per His Excellency's instructions, the foreigners had been placed under twenty-four-hour surveillance, but (and His Excellency would please forgive his raising this problem a second time) he was obliged to confess that the surveillance was, in effect, from the aural point of view, quite deaf.

He checked his last sentence against the informer's report, and his contentment at having found such a happy formulation evaporated instantly. Apart from the expression "Your Excellency," which had replaced "the governor" in Dull's version, his sentence was in all respects identical to his agent's words. He realized he had become enslaved by Dull's style. "To hell with the whole business!" he sighed, suddenly exhausted. He had begun to ponder something else. Should he ask the minister to send an English-speaking informer, or would it be better not to annoy him with a request of that kind? When he had raised the question in one of his letters a fortnight ago, the minister's office had refused point-blank: there were only two English-speaking operatives in Tirana, one of whom barely managed to cover the British Legation, and the other had an ear infection and was thus, in effect, unavailable. Under the circumstances, the ministry wrote, the governor would have to accept that however important it might be to keep a close watch on the foreigners, he could not have the services of the only currently active English-speaking agent in the capital. The office would try to find one for him from some other part of the kingdom, but the governor should take note here and now that it would be no easy task, because quite apart from the shortage of intelligence operatives with foreign languages, the whole issue of informers had recently been complicated by the results of a medical survey, which showed that for years a number of agents had been hiding the fact that their hearing was very poor.

The governor cursed himself for not having taken the initiative in encouraging Dull Baxhaja to learn some English. Added to his other skills, he would certainly have made a better job of it. Had he not managed to learn a bit of Latin in double-quick time when he'd had to spy on the Bishop of Shkodër's conversations with local priests? And on top of that, hadn't he learned to speak Romany almost fluently in order to help track down a horse that had been stolen from the king's stables?

Well, he sighed, to comfort himself, how can you know where the next foreigner is going to come from? You may get geared up for an Englishman, but how do you know it won't be a Turkish tourist or a Japanese visitor or God knows what else who turns up next on your doorstep? It really was a devilishly tricky business.

His eyes wandered back to Dull's report. The conclusion was a real masterpiece, and the governor was sorry not to be able to quote it verbatim in his letter to the minister. "Look, he's bringing up the English issue again, damn him," the governor exclaimed. What if he concluded his report without explicitly raising the language question again but referring nonetheless to the awkwardness of "deaf" surveillance, in other words of relying solely on the visual observation of suspects? That would provide the opportunity for transcribing every word of Dull's philosophical reflections on the relationship between the eye and the ear in the trade or craft of surveillance.

The governor reread his informer's paragraphs before putting pen to paper. Masterful! he thought, in utter amazement at the skill of the phrasing. It's Shakespeare and Dante rolled into one! "For as the governor will know," Dull had written, "spying is above all an art of the ear. The support of the eye is only a secondary, not to say superfluous, issue. Besides, all the great spies had poor eyesight, not to mention those who were quite simply blind."

"What a capital fellow!" the governor mumbled. "No two ways about it, he's the devil himself." And so he began to copy out what Dull had written.

5

WHERE AM I? HE WONDERED. How did I get here? Clumps of hair brushed against his chin, then on his nose, and as he opened his eyes with a start, he nearly screamed in terror, thinking he saw the long russet fur of his childhood teddy bear or toy fox nearly burying his face. But he quickly got a grip on himself and pushed back the blanket that had worked its way over his head in the night.

Day was breaking. The dawn's gray light trickled in through the half-open shutter of one of the room's narrow windows. The misted pane gave an even more ashen hue to the light. Bill turned toward Max's bed and saw that his friend was still asleep.

The Buffalo . . . , he mused. So here they were on a gray winter's morning in this legendary inn, where you went to bed under those thick, long-haired blankets that are indigenous to the Balkans. Their adventure had truly begun. There was no turning back now, even if they had wanted to give up. Brrr! It was freezing! But the low temperature was bracing and filled him with joy. Getting out of bed slowly and carefully so as to make as little noise as possible, he stepped daintily across the creaking and groaning boards to the window. His eyes rested on a low sky that seemed to have had its heart torn out by some unknown cataclysm.

The smell of roasted coffee wafted up from below. It must be time to get up, he thought, and he dressed and descended to the ground floor.

"Good morning, sir," said the innkeeper, who loomed suddenly before him. "Did you sleep well?"

"Good morning. . . . Yes, very well, thank you."

Bill noticed on his right a door that opened onto a ground-floor room piled high with bunks, crammed side by side. Most of them were empty, but in two or three of them you could make out shapes wrapped in heavy blankets.

"The main quarters," the innkeeper explained. "That is the way in all the inns in this region. All of them have large common sleeping quarters, and one or two private rooms for special visitors, such as yourselves. You see, folks are very poor in these parts."

"I understand."

A few minutes later, he was walking along the road that wound its way across the plain. The bushes by the wayside were laced with frost. A hedgerow or two, no doubt planted so as to mark off the land that belonged to the inn, passed to his rear as he walked, leaving him completely alone and undisturbed. "What peace!" Bill muttered. That was an understatement. It was no ordinary peacefulness. A thrush's song underlined the otherwise total silence. But the high-pitched screech was not prompted solely by his footfalls. It seemed more like the sign of some unseen agitation, as if, for some reason, dream beings had decided to disport themselves on this very plain.

Bill felt an unaccustomed eagerness and energy welling up inside him. All of a sudden, at this early-morning hour, everything seemed possible. He felt he was strong enough to tackle the problems of the universe, to alter the length of the day, to change the seasons' rhythm, indeed to correct the rotation of the earth on its axis. As for Homeric poetry, he would solve that puzzle, easy as pie.

He did not know how long he had been walking along in such a mood. Turning around, he saw the inn in the far distance. Max must be up, he thought.

By the time Bill got back, Max was indeed downstairs, drinking coffee with the innkeeper.

After eating breakfast, the two men went out together and took the same road Bill had walked on earlier. It was still as peaceful, but Bill noticed that the inner joy that he had felt had faded. The edges of the plain were blanketed in fog. Now and again a few black birds would swoop out from the mist as from another world, coast low over the plain, and then vanish into thin air like ghosts. Two or three times they thought they could make out the peaks of Bjeshkët e Nemuna, the Accursed Mountains, through the fog.

They had talked of them so often in New York and throughout their journey that they were now dying of impatience to see them. Their original plan had involved starting their research with a trek up into the mountains, but when they learned that winters there were really hard, that the cols were almost impassable, and that living conditions on the heights were extremely rough, they thought better of it. All the people they had managed to contact who knew anything about northern Albania persuaded them that they would stand a much better chance of meeting rhapsodes at a place where several roads met, such as the Buffalo Inn, than in any of the few hamlets they might encounter on a trek through the mountains.

The previous evening, the innkeeper had assured them that *lahuta* players did stop over at his inn at least twice in every month. In the old days it was different, he had said with a sigh; we had singers here almost every night. But it seemed that those days were gone forever. Anyway, they should not worry: they would definitely meet some rhapsodes.

Despite being determined to keep their secret to the last, they had realized that they could not avoid confiding in the innkeeper. So without more ado, they had tried to explain it all to him as clearly as they could.

"I understand what you are saying, gentlemen." He nodded, moving his head in the same way as he did when ordering coffee from the kitchen. "I understand you perfectly. It's as if my inn had been built with your work in mind. Especially for listening twice to the same rhapsode. A rhapsode who spends a night here will come back a week later, at the most two weeks later, on his way home from a wedding, or a funeral, or from a murder he has gone to commit. For there is no other way back to the Rrafsh, there's no other road. Unless you have wings . . . But in winter even the birds can't fly over the Accursed Mountains."

The innkeeper had just one reservation: would the rhapsodes agree to sing in front of the machine? He had told the visitors how a *lahuta* player always performs with a degree of ceremony and ritual, and only when there is a good-size audience. But they should not worry even on that score. On winter nights his inn often had a real party atmosphere. He would do all he could to make sure they were not disappointed. He would light the fire in the great hearth in the common quarters and ply the rhapsode with raki; and as for the recording machine, well, let's see what happens. They might decide to explain what it was to the *lahuta* players, or else play a simple trick, like covering it with a sheepskin. But anyway, they were not to worry, it would turn out all right.

Bill and Max thought back to all these confident assurances as they strode across the plain. They really could not have hoped to fall in with an innkeeper better suited to help them in their work. He was a keen follower of the rhapsodes, he knew the epic singers' ways like the back of his hand, he knew their weak spots and their itineraries. He was a living encyclopedia of bard lore. And what's more, he talked about it with passionate admiration. He would mention the seasonal variations in the frequency of the rhapsodes' visits as if he were speaking about migrating birds. Even the vocabulary he used to talk of the singers was delicate, full of affectionate suffixes spoken so softly as to make you sigh. They really had had a stroke of luck in coming across an innkeeper like that.

As they chatted, they looked upward from time to

time in the hope of making out the peaks of Bjeshkët e Nemuna on the far horizon, but the vast flat plain was still surrounded by fog. All the same, you could sense the bulk of the great plateau that began over there, not so far away, really. They were in the heart of the epic zone whose magnetism had attracted them from across the ocean. The Homeric puzzle they were trying to solve must be blanketed in the same thick fog. But Bill's feelings having changed from an hour before, he no longer thought that he and Max could succeed. They were so small and powerless, maybe they were condemned to wander forever on the edge of the ghostly realm, never able to enter it. He could hardly suppress a deep sigh.

"Look over there!" Max shouted suddenly. "Are those men, or am I having visions?"

"You're asking me? You know very well that . . ."

Max cupped his hand on his brow. "They're men, all right," he confirmed. "Couldn't be more normal, and yet, I don't know, I had an odd feeling."

Bill figured he wouldn't see anything whatsoever emerge from the pea soup on the plain. But the black dots that had crossed the line between the two realms were indeed coming closer. Their alarm made the two friends realize why they had doubted whether they would ever find any human beings, let alone singers of epics as in ancient times, in these bleak uplands. Even if any were left, they must surely be half frozen already, at death's door, and likely to disappear before another winter or two had passed. That is why the two of them had had to hurry, to get there before it was too late, so as to grab the key to the mystery from the rhapsodes' last gasp.

Neither had confided his doubts to the other, so as not to depress themselves further at the hardest times, when obstacles had seemed to be in league with each other to prevent their journey to Albania. But they had got over their gloomy patches and now, as if to reward them for their perseverance, it seemed, the mountains were presenting them with living beings, who were walking toward them. They kept quiet until the men were very close. It was their first encounter with highlanders from the true epic zone. Their dress was identical to the descriptions they had read in ancient epic poetry, and they almost shouted with astonishment: How is it that they have not changed a thing in a thousand years? Their black cloaks had shoulder pads decorated with truncated or atrophied winglets that made you shiver. Looking on these highlanders, you were looking at the boundary between men and gods, the watershed, the point of contact or of separation, depending on how you wanted to see it. Epic poetry spoke of them; there was even an old Albanian word to describe them, *hyanjeri,* or "god-man," presumably without equivalent in any language except ancient Greek. The black cloak fell over long, narrow trousers the color of milk, with a dotted black zigzag line down the side, roughly the shape of the symbol for high-voltage electricity. Max and Bill had never seen a costume like it: as if the robes of a medieval monk had been combined with the tunic a ballet dancer might wear to represent Evil onstage. The Irishmen thought they could see something Illyrian about the highlanders' dress, as well as a touch of Balkan gloom, alongside something else, reminiscent of Scottish highland attire or of the denizens of those high glacial plateaus that remain unmapped by men.

"Woodcutters," Max whispered, when he noticed that the highlanders carried ax blades on their backs. They definitely were woodcutters, and the Irishmen were all the more sure of it because they knew that Albanians never use sharp weapons to settle scores: their rules of conduct allow that only the bullet be used for dispatching enemies. Yes, definitely woodcutters, Bill repeated to himself. All the same, those blades looked as if they could easily have been stained with the dried blood of very ancient crimes.

The highlanders drew near. Some of their features called to mind the silhouettes that you find on classical vases. But the way the men walked was not quite like a normal marching stride, for their gait had been formed and modeled by the *kanun.*

"Hail!" said the first highlander.

The greeting took the scholars aback, and at first they gaped in silence. Bill then managed to utter a composite version of "good morning" and *mirëdita.* As for Max, he just made a gesture of greeting.

After a while the Irishmen turned around and realized that they had gone so far from the inn as to have lost it from view. On their way back, they made firm resolutions to get down to work without delay — the next day at the latest, and even sooner, if a bard should come by that evening.

All was quiet at the Buffalo Inn. They went up to

their room and opened their trunks to fish out more file cards and maps. The only wall spaces left for their notes and maps were over the fireplace and between the two windows (though the latter space was not really big enough).

"Do we have mice?" Max suddenly asked aloud, raising his eyes to the ceiling.

Bill, who was unfolding a map of the Balkans, stopped and looked up as well.

"I don't think so."

He looked at the map, on which the mountain ranges looked like horses' ribs strewn in disarray on the flagstones of a slaughterhouse. The lettering over them read: "Northern Albania," "Rrafsh," "Kosovo," "Old Serbia."

For more than a thousand years, Albanians and Slavs had been in ceaseless conflict in this area. They had quarreled over everything — over land, over boundaries, over pastures and watering holes — and it would have been entirely unsurprising had they also disputed the ownership of local rainbows. And as if that were not enough, they also squabbled over the ancient epics, which existed, just to make things completely intractable, in both languages, Albanian and Serbo-Croatian. Each of the two peoples asserted that it had created the epic, leaving the other nation the choice of being considered either a thief or a mere imitator.

"Did it ever occur to you that whether we like it or not, our work on Homer plunges us into this conflict?" Bill said without raising his eyes from the map.

"Do you think so?"

"It's virtually inevitable. What we are trying to prove is that the material from which Albanian epic poetry is made is Homeric in origin; that would not be possible if the Albanians had not been here since classical times; and what arouses the jealousy and anger of the Serbs is precisely the question of historical precedence in the occupation of the Balkan peninsula."

"I see . . . Jealousy . . . ," Max muttered.

The rows he had had with his wife in New York just before leaving had been utterly depressing. "Buzz off, the two of you, go wherever you want with your mistress. Clear out, I said! Run off with that skirt-chaser Bill Norton! Only don't try to pull the wool over my eyes with all that Homeric nonsense! Don't you realize just how ridiculous you are?"

"Are you listening?" Bill asked.

"Sure, sure . . . You were saying something about jealousy. . . ."

"Right. The Serbs just can't accept that the Albanians were here before they were. Throughout the Balkans, local nationalisms like this give rise to absurd and morbid passions, but since this one relates to the Kosovo question, it also has a concrete political implication."

Bill, still poring over the map, looked worried.

"A thousand-year war," he said dreamily. "That's an awfully long time, isn't it?"

"Too long. But it's war that gives birth to epic poetry," said Max, turning toward the trunks. "It's bloodthirsty stuff."

For a moment they stared at the cold and gleaming

metal cases. The task they had set themselves was to pack into those trunks the entirety of the epic poetry spread around the high plateau of the Rrafsh.

"The Germans called this a racial war," Max said. "They even made it plain they considered the Albanians the superior race."

"I grant you we're dealing with a nasty conflict," Bill concurred. "But when I hear people talk of race, and especially of superior and inferior races, well, I just blow up. To me that stinks of Nazism."

"All the same, it's a very fashionable concept these days."

They fell silent.

"The others also wanted to take their epic away from them," said Bill finally, turning from his map.

"Of course," said Max. "When you take over a whole house, you aren't squeamish about stealing all the treasures it contains."

"Epic poetry is murderous stuff!" Bill exclaimed, and he stared again at the trunks as if the epic itself were inside, about to brim over at any minute.

"It's chilly," said Max, rubbing his hands.

He put down his notes and wrapped himself in the big blanket. Then Bill did the same. They were shivering, and gradually they yielded to a feeling of numbness.

Bill propped his head on the pillow and tried to imagine the Slavs' first incursion into the Balkans. Albanian epics occasionally mentioned it, alluding to the countless waves of men from the north and northeast, and the slow retreat before them, mile by mile, of the longer-standing populations of the peninsula. It seemed the Slav tide would never stop; unlike the Roman invasion, the conquest was achieved without armies, flags, or treaties. It must have been an unending straggle of women and children moving forward to the muddled sounds of yelling and squalling, a cohort obeying no orders, leaving no milestones or monuments, more like a natural disaster than a military invasion. That was the shock that disturbed the Balkans most, he figured, especially the Albanians of yore. All of a sudden they were in the midst of a Slavic sea: a gray, unending, anonymous Eurasian mass that could easily destroy all the treasures of a land where art had flourished more than anywhere else on earth. So what had to happen happened: the people who had lived here for centuries took up arms and bloodied the shores of the ocean. And the waves were held back at the very shores of Kosovo.

There was a knock at the door.

"Come in!" said Max.

It was Shtjefen, with an armful of firewood.

"Would you like me to light a fire?" he asked. "The cold is really coming on."

"Oh, thank you! We were chatting about the enmity between Serbs and Albanians. Are things as bad as people say?"

"They are probably even worse than you think," Shtjefen said as he laid the logs on the hearth. "Do you know what an Albanian poet wrote? 'We were born to mutual anger . . .'"

"A poet wrote that?"

"Yes, sir."

"'We were born to mutual anger,' " Bill repeated.

"There's that word *anger,* or *resentment,* again, just like at the beginning of the *Iliad.* . . . "

The memory of the Albanian diplomat in Washington flashed across their minds.

"Are there any mice here?" Max asked distractedly.

"That's not the first time it seemed to me that . . ."

"We disinfested the inn especially for you, sir."

The fire blazed up quickly. Shtjefen left and the two scholars continued talking, pacing up and down the room or standing with their backs to the fireplace, their hands spread out to catch the warmth.

They spent the whole afternoon sorting out their notes and file cards. Outside, the light was failing by the minute, and there came a time when their conversation flagged. On this late winter's afternoon, they felt completely cut off, swaddled in silence, in a faraway inn. Would every day be the same?

Max was the first to think how to shake off the encroaching gloom: he lit the oil lamp, whose beam kept at bay the somber dusk that had now covered the face of the world outside like a death mask.

6

THE FIRST RHAPSODE put in at the Buffalo Inn four days later. Windswept rain rattling the shutters had been getting on the Irishmen's nerves. When Shtjefen appeared in the doorway, they realized from the expression on his face that their keenest wish had been granted.

"He's downstairs," the innkeeper whispered, as if imparting a secret.

The rhapsode was on his way to a different part of the country on personal business; he would come back by the same route in a fortnight; if Shtjefen had understood the scholars correctly, this was exactly the kind of circumstance they were seeking in order to record twice over the singing of the same bard.

"*Lahuta* players are not easygoing people," Shtjefen continued, "and it wasn't simple to persuade this one to stay. 'It's dreadful weather,' I told him, 'and it's getting late. Believe me, I have no stake in this, and of course you'll get free lodging. I've got only one request to make . . . ,' and that's when I told him about you two."

In the common quarters on the ground floor, there

sat a handful of highlanders, all soaked to the skin. Before making out which of them was the rhapsode, the scholars noticed the *lahuta* propped against the wall. Then Shtjefen put his hand on the shoulder of one of the men (just at the spot where the cut-off ribbons were sewn to his cloak), and the man turned around. They reached agreement on the spot. The rhapsode looked hard at one of the foreigners for a long moment, seemingly to remove a doubt from his mind. The Irishmen had rarely seen eyes so fair or so piercing, with what seemed like a crack running through them, as if they were staring through a broken mirror. The innkeeper kept talking to the rhapsode, who did not appear to be listening, but then he lowered his head sharply, a gesture signifying yes. In accordance with ancient custom, he would not accept any reward. It was understood only that he would not pay for his night at the inn.

Getting the tape recorder downstairs was a troublesome business, just as getting it up to the room in the first place had been. The highlanders watching from the ground floor were intrigued.

Night had fallen, and Shtjefen lit the tall oil lamp, the one used for important occasions. There was a special, party atmosphere at the inn this evening. Only the rhapsode, who was aware of being the hero of the night, stood aside, looking calmly at the tape recorder. Bill kept glancing at him, trying to imagine what feelings this ultramodern device aroused in the rhapsode: bewilderment? apprehension? guilt about betraying his predecessors, the singers of yore? In the end, he concluded that the rhapsode's calm masked inner turmoil. It would be the first time that the sound of his voice and of his *lahuta* would not be lost to the air, as sounds had always been, but instead would be collected inside this metal box, like rainwater in a cistern or like . . . He suddenly feared that the rhapsode might change his mind.

Bill was reassured by the sight of the company, sitting in a semicircle, mostly on the floor. The ritual had already begun, and nothing and nobody would halt it now.

At last the rhapsode took up his *lahuta*. It made a monotonous sound that seemed to draw the listener on into some all-embracing dream. Bill and Max glanced at each other. The rhapsode began to sing, in a voice quite unlike his speaking voice. It was unnatural, cold, unwavering, full of an anguish that seemed to come from another world. It made Bill's spine tingle. He tried to follow the meaning of the words, but the monotonous delivery of the singer made that impossible. It felt as if he were being emptied from inside, as if his guts were being drawn out of him, as if his inner being were slowly being wound along a woolen thread turning on a distaff. The rhapsode's voice had the ability to hollow you out. If he went on much longer, everyone here was going to dissolve on the spot. But the *lahuta* stopped in time.

In the sudden silence, the tape machine's soft purring could be heard, and it was Max who reached out a hand to switch it off. Then the crowd came back to life, as if emerging from a trance. Congratulations came from every side. Bill and Max chimed in with their thank-yous in Albanian, but they sounded weak indeed alongside the ritual formulations the highlanders lavished on the rhapsode.

Before the rhapsode began his second song, Max checked the quality of the recording. When the machine reproduced the rhapsode's voice, a little more resonant that it had seemed on first hearing, everyone was struck dumb. The man was there, with his mouth shut and his *lahuta* at rest, yet you could hear the sound of his voice and of his instrument. There was something quite horrifying about this disconnection, this removal of a man from the attributes that gave him his distinct and independent existence.

They all huddled around the machine and gaped at the two reels, turning like a pair of grinding wheels. Their eyes were full of questions they did not dare to put into words. So the voice was now stored inside the box, but in what form?

After a short interval, the rhapsode sang a second ballad.

"Won't the two songs get muddled inside there?" one of the traveling highlanders asked in the end, pointing to the machine.

Bill tried not to laugh aloud.

It was late at night before they switched off the tape recorder and thanked the rhapsode.

"In a fortnight," Shtjefen told him, "when you pass by here again, you'll sing the same songs. As I told you, that's what interests these gentlemen. They want to make comparisons, and I'm not sure what else. Besides, you gave me your word as a man, and you'll keep it."

"Fear not," said the singer in a somber tone.

"So the voice can be kept in there for a fortnight?" asked one young highlander. "It doesn't rust?"

"Not a bit," Bill replied. "It can stay in there for months, even years."

The *lahuta* player was staring hard at the case of the recorder. From the glow in the man's eyes, Bill reckoned that there was something troubling him. What if he changes his mind? Bill wondered anxiously. What if he has found it a bad omen to leave his voice locked and trapped in a box?

The two foreigners bade good night to all and went back up to their room. Shtjefen, for his part, put out the oil lamp and left the large room in darkness.

Bill felt as if the troubled and fitful sleep of the ground-floor guests had followed the two of them upstairs. Tomorrow, he thought — as if he needed to fasten his mind on something clearer and more logical in order to dispel a profound sense of fear caused by he knew not what — tomorrow we'll have our work cut out! He wrapped himself in his blanket and gave a deep sigh.

Bill woke several times in the night, thinking it was dawn, but each time sunrise seemed to be ever further off. When finally he woke up properly, it was quite late.

Going downstairs, the Irishmen discovered with surprise that the main quarters of the inn were entirely deserted.

"They've gone," Shtjefen said when he noticed their amazement. "Highland folk get up very early." Through the open door you could see the dark, rain-heavy sky.

"And just think," the innkeeper continued, "they're traveling in that weather!"

The clack of Martin's clogs could be heard, then the lad himself appeared at the back door, a bucket of water in each hand.

"Morning," he said.

"Good morning, Martin. Did you have a good night?" asked Max.

"Hmm . . . So-so . . . I was worried about . . . about the recorder. . . ."

"Why so?" Bill queried.

"Well, how should I know?" he stammered. "Anything could happen, couldn't it?"

Martin's face looked vaguely worried, and Bill remembered his own bad night and the anxiety that had seemed to rise from below, as if it were coming from another age. . . .

February 27,
at the Inn of the Bone of the Buffalo

Today we really began our work on the Homeric enigma.

We listened several times to the two poems sung by the rhapsode last night. Each song has about a thousand lines.

We compared both of them to the published versions, and as we expected, we found significant variations.

The first one tells of the treachery of Ajkuna, wife of the valiant Muj. German scholars saw her as a kind of Helen of Troy of Albanian epic. Except that her story is enough to make your blood curdle.

The other song must be a version of the epic of Zuk the Standard Bearer. It would be hard to think up a more tragic tale. A young woman is in the mountains, looking for her brother, who has been mortally wounded by his enemies. She finds him at last, drowning in his own blood. The wounded man asks for a drink, but there is no spring near at hand, and she is afraid that if she leaves him, she would not find her way back; so he tells her to soak a strip of cloth from her dress in his blood and let it drip as she walks, to mark her route; she follows his advice, but the rain comes and washes away the drops of blood. She loses her way and wanders around the mountains until she is confronted by a crow and a bear. The crow confesses that he has just picked out the eyes of a wounded man, and the bear admits he gobbled up the man's head; so she flees, screaming, across the fog-enshrouded mountain.

"How horrible!" Max exclaimed when he turned off the recording.

We spent the rest of the day transcribing this ballad. No doubt we'll spend more days on it.

Late February,
at the Inn of the Bone of the Buffalo

We're waiting with impatience, not to say anxiety, for the rhapsode to come back.

Sometimes we are frightened of burying ourselves in the world of the epic and losing sight of the main aim of our visit. We are Homeric scholars. That's what we keep telling ourselves, every day, reminding ourselves that we came here not to study the Albanians' epic poetry but to try to solve the enigma of Homer.

Easier said than done. In spite of ourselves, epic absorbs us. And then we encounter issues that are more tangled than grass roots. For example, we have now identified two other versions of the adventures of Ajkuna, wife of Muj, and they give quite different explanations for what happened to her. It must have been the same with the rape of Helen in pre-Homeric poems — until Homer came along and chose one of the variants.

The Homeric account itself implies that there had been various different earlier views of Helen's position. The whole story of the rape of the queen is deeply ambiguous. Did she follow Paris of her own free will, or was she taken by force before she fell in love with him? Maybe she never did love her violator but was just his slave! Alternatively, was she first fascinated by Paris, then, when tricked, did her feelings abate? Or was it rather he who first fell in love with her, then felt his passion waning, which is not exactly a rare event in such circumstances?

Homer manages to keep all these questions in the air. He never gives a final answer, neither during the Trojan War nor afterward, when the enigma of Helen's absconding ought to be explained. All you find is a degree of remorse for all that happened, and that sentiment is, moreover, spread rather thin. As for her behavior toward Menelaus, her lawful husband, that too is hardly transparent: we do not know if she hated him, despised him, or loved him.

Though each of them recounts Ajkuna's position variantly, the different versions of the Albanian ballad are, individually, clear and straightforward. In one version, Ajkuna is carried off into slavery by Muj's Slav rival and, like any prisoner, spends her time waiting for her release from captivity. But there is another version, where the kidnapper is so fascinated by her that he turns her into a princess. Not only does he abandon his wife, but he forces her to hold a torch between her teeth to illuminate the first night of his love-making with Ajkuna. This variant does not mention

Ajkuna's own feelings; but in two other versions, those feelings are clearly delineated. In one, despite being made a princess, Ajkuna remains faithful to her first husband; in the other, she falls in love with her kidnapper as soon as she is carried off, and furthermore, when Muj comes to rescue her, she cheats on him heartlessly. That was the version the rhapsode had sung — where Muj is betrayed, is chained to the lovers' bed, and has a flaming pine branch forced between his teeth, illuminating the lovers' pleasure.

It is obvious that each of the four Ajkunas overlaps with a part of Helen of Troy, or rather that Helen of Troy is an amalgam of these four different figures. As Homer depicts her, Helen is a rather muddled character, and the behavior of Menelaus is no less a confusion.

March 1,
at the Inn of the Bone of the Buffalo

This sun shines brightly but gives little warmth. . . .

It is cold, but we are contented. We have ended up discovering the foundations of a common Greco-Illyrian-Albanian proto-universe. Medieval Albanian poets went on asserting its existence for hundreds of years, but as is often the way with poets, they made themselves heard only when it was too late.

We're trying to put ourselves inside Homer's skin to understand what kind of tyrannical power he must have had to contain such a bubbling cauldron of artistic activity.

The old worries still surface from time to time: are we going to get lost in the maelstrom? And another, more material worry: is the first rhapsode going to come back?

March 3, at the Inn

We were counting the hours until our lahuta player was due back, and then two other rhapsodes arrived, unannounced. We were really in luck, Shtjefen told us; it had been a long while since so many singers were seen in the space of a few days. One of the singers was placid and not at all talkative, like all the highlanders, but the other was a nervous, jumpy fellow. Always getting up and sitting down, going to the door, watching the road as if he was expecting something, good news or bad. Oddly enough, after Shtjefen had discussed matters with the rhapsodes, it was the jumpy one who agreed to sing for the two foreigners.

Contrary to expectations, he declared that he would sing without accompanying himself on the lahuta. *He did not explain why. Was the string of his instrument broken? Or his hand not in good shape? Everyone fell silent around him, like the last time, but before starting to chant, the rhapsode raised his right arm, opened his hand wide, and placed the flat palm on his cheekbone, beside his ear. His outstretched fingers appeared to be sticking out from the back of his head, like a crest or comb — and Bill and I both muttered in astonishment,* Majekrah *(wing tip)! We had just seen, right before our eyes, the ancient ritual gesture with its untranslatable name that we knew about from the scholarly literature.*

There was a long silence before the bard began his chant. He started by declaiming these lines:

Today I shall reclaim an ancient debt of blood —
No one else on earth has ever reclaimed so much . . .

Max and I shouted out in unison, "It's the ballad of Zuk the Standard Bearer!"

And indeed it was that entrancing ballad he sang, and what's more, in its full version. We had dreamed of hearing this poem ever since we first got interested in Albanian epic. Not for nothing have German scholars called it the Albanian Oresteia. *It has all the elements of ancient drama: a mother's betrayal, a sister inciting her brother to matricide, and Furies, and retribution. . . .*

When he had finished, we asked the rhapsode when he would be back, but to our great surprise (and to Shtjefen's surprise, above all), he replied that he would never return to the Rrafsh.

Shtjefen was struck dumb by the answer. A highlander leaving the plateau forever was unthinkable, and worse still, it was a bad omen, a sign of terrible misfortunes to come.

"We live in bad times," said Shtjefen. "The worst things can happen."

March

The inn is empty. We keep working, but now and again our spirits sink. The first rhapsode has not reappeared.

His coming back is of vital importance to us. We are sure of recording and rerecording the singing of other rhapsodes, but if the first one doesn't return, it will feel like an emotional hurt, like the wound that first love makes in your heart.

Shtjefen keeps glancing at us guiltily. It's obvious that he is more upset than we are about the long wait. Sometimes he goes out onto the doorstep and peers at the road as

*it disappears into the fog. It isn't a view
that inspires optimism, especially when it's
raining.*

*Yesterday there was an unusual noise when
we were downstairs drinking our morning
coffee. A distant thrumming. We went outside to have a look. Shtjefen also came out
and looked up into the sky.*

*"It's a civilian airplane, which overflies this
area twice a month," he said.*

"With passengers?"

*Bill and I exchanged glances, and our looks
of suspicion did not escape Shtjefen, who
came up to us and whispered:*

*"Don't worry. Up there" — he made a
vague gesture to where the noise was coming
from — "in the Rrafsh, there are no airports,
and even if there were, no highlander would
ever get on board an airplane."*

"Oh, really?" said Max. "And why not?"

*"There are lots of reasons, believe me,"
Shtjefen answered. "But one will be enough
for you: the price of a plane ticket would
come to two or three years of a highlander's
income."*

We nodded to indicate that we understood.

*"Therefore he will return, without fail,"
Shtjefen went on, accentuating each word.
Then his voice faltered. "Unless . . . unless he
is dead."*

7

*I*N FACT, THE INNKEEPER'S PREDICTION was borne out, and the rhapsode did return. It happened on a muffled, darkly overcast day. Everything seemed to be frozen still and the singing forgotten forever. The man looked so worn out that the Irishmen wondered what could have happened to him, but they did not dare ask. They did not even hope to hear the man sing again; they asked the innkeeper not to remind the traveler of his promise, but Shtjefen shook his head in disagreement: the rhapsode would sing without fail; he had given his word. And he did indeed keep his promise. Without saying anything, as if fulfilling a duty, he took his place in a wooden chair in front of the microphone and began to chant first the one, then the other of the two ballads.

As soon as the rhapsode had left, Bill and Max started to compare the new recording with their transcription of the original performance, and they went on until late in the evening and again on the next day. They had thought that with his ashen face, the exhausted bard would have modified the words quite a lot. As a heading to the tape, Max recorded himself saying in English: "Ballad sung two weeks later by the same rhapsode, who appears to have suffered a psychological shock or deep distress in the meantime."

However, to their acute astonishment, they discovered that the two texts were to all intents and purposes identical. In one thousand lines of verse, there were only two omissions; and in the scene where Muj is chained up, the line

The remains of the burnt pinewood
blackened Muj's chin

was reformulated as

The burnt remains of the pinewood mingled
with the foam from his mouth

The two of them discussed the reasons for this change at some length. On the one hand, it seemed that this tiny alteration and the omission of two lines out of a thousand were the very least of the losses that might be expected; on the other hand, the change could be accounted for by the singer's low spirits adding to the bitterness of his song.

Then they set that explanation aside, feeling it to be quite secondary, and looked more closely at the altered line. It was amazing. They had before their eyes their first, long-awaited free variant! There it was, not as a theoretical construct but as a real and living thing. The omission of two lines, that tiny void in the text, was the first example of forgetting that they had pinned down alive. They were fascinated and did not tire of examining both the variant and the absent lines, and suddenly everything seemed possible. They had in their hands one of the main threads of the Homeric tangle: what happened with a single rhapsode in a fortnight. Over several years, or a century, or five hundred years, how many instances of forgetting would there be, and not just in a single rhapsode's performances but in a whole series of them, over a generation, and from one generation to the next? The device of forgetting suddenly grew to huge and striking size, and they could feel their pulses throbbing in their temples as they tried to get their brains to cope with such vast dimensions.

They were completely buried in their work when they got an invitation to a ball to be given by the governor and his wife. At first they did not really understand what it was about, since the approach seemed so peculiar, out of place, irrelevant, so pointless and absurd. Both said "No!" instinctively. "What use is that to us? It must be a mistake." Unable to get used to the idea that they had indeed been invited to a dance, they persuaded themselves that it must be a mix-up and that the invitation cards were really intended for someone else. However, their own names were handwritten on the invitation cards. Moreover, the governor's long-nosed limousine was parked right there in front of the inn. Not only had they been invited to a ball; they had been assigned a car to take them there! They were about to reiterate their refusal, when they vaguely remembered that there had been some talk of a ball at the soiree they attended on their first night in N —— and that in addition this whole area and maybe the inns and some of the itinerant singers came under the governor's jurisdiction. . . .

Half an hour later, dressed up in their dark suits, they were being chauffeured in an antiquated jalopy across a darkening, frosted plain that seemed strewn with enigmas. Here and there ghostly haystacks tried to duck under the headlights. Now and again Bill muttered under his breath, "Oh Lord, where are we going?" He needed to think hard to remind himself that they were on their way to the local governor's ball, but no sooner had he come to his senses than his imagination raced again, inventing a thousand hidden dangers all around, long smothered by the ice but now reluctantly, and all the more distressingly, awakening from their slumbers.

He heard Max whisper into his ear: "I've never seen such a sunset!"

It was indeed a unique sunset, spread across an ink-black sky swept clean of every speck of stardust, every source of light, all hint of softness. A fine night to be kidnapped! thought Bill. The governor's wife — or her husband — with a torch between her or his teeth (depending on which rhapsode's version you listened to) . . . oh, those epics could set your nerves on edge!

Bill sighed with relief when he could make out the twinkling lights of the little town in the distance. Lanterns burned brightly at the door of the governor's house. In the salon they found the same guests as on their first visit, and some new faces as well, presumably representing local high society.

"We are delighted to see you among us once again," said the governor as he introduced them to the other guests. "The local gynecologist . . . The lawyer and his wife . . . Mr. Rrok — but you know him already, don't you . . . And the postmaster too. It is really a great pleasure to have you back. The head of the regional recruitment office . . . And this is my wife."

The scholars felt just as foreign after an hour in the place as they had on first arriving. Like everyone else, they had glasses in their hands, they had even had a dance (just one), but they could not feel part of anything in that environment. It all seemed made of cardboard, as false as it was ridiculous. They realized how impossible it was to tear oneself away from the world of epic poetry and behave as one should at a ball. Women whispering in corners kept looking at them sideways, presumably gossiping about them, but that didn't matter. The two foreigners felt miles away; they were still at the inn, where the people, and their clothes, and their gestures, and their code of conduct, were so different. . . .

Leaning against the marble mantelpiece, Bill cast his mind back to the travelers who had stayed at the inn, their costumes decorated with designs suggestive of snow or frost, decorations that seemed to have been put on by a machine able to embroider the pattern of lightning.

As for the folk sitting around the governor's salon, the alleged elite of the town of N——, well, they were just straw men, ridiculous bureaucrats. They made you want to laugh, or be sick.

The hostess sidled up to Bill and said, "You don't look as though you're quite at your ease. Of course you're bored. This is the end of the world, so what can you expect?"

"But of course not, madam," Bill said, not really knowing how to respond.

To tell the truth, she was the only person in the whole pantomime who seemed to be different, and he did not want to offend her.

Her bright, submissive, and liquid eyes came close, appearing to bear the mark of the last weeks' separation. Even the ring that sparkled on the hand that held the glass seemed to have acquired some of its mistress's yearning.

Bill could smell her perfume, and he suddenly felt like blurting out the question: How could two Albanias coexist, in the same place, in the same period, when they were so completely different — eternal Albania, bearing its tragic destiny with dignity, as he had come to know it not only from its epic poetry but also at the inn up there, beside the main road; and the other Albania, the one he could see here and (he was sorry, but he had to be blunt) that struck him as nothing more than a dumb show.

"You're dreaming . . . ," she said. "You say nothing and you dream. But I have a weakness for people like that. . . ."

"I *am* a little perplexed," Bill replied. "In fact, I was about to ask you a question."

He thought he saw the ring on her finger quiver. Maybe she would not understand what he meant. It was quite possible that she knew absolutely nothing of the other Albania. Actually, anyone could well doubt its existence. Was old Albania really the way he saw it, or was his vision of it only a poet's reverie?

He picked up the glass he had left on the mantelpiece, took a sip, and put it down again. A piece he had read by a young Albanian writer claimed that the highlanders, who appeared to be so valiant and rebellious, were capable of giving in overnight and of crawling before the power of the state. Seen from a greater distance, however, things looked very different. There was nothing really surprising about it. Did people of the Homeric period behave in epic fashion? And what about Homer himself . . . ? A horrible vision (as when you see yourself sleeping with your own mother) had seized upon his mind and would not go away: Homer, having just finished chanting the second or the seventh book of the *Iliad,* completely obsessed with counting out his pay . . . He had been delivered from this agonizing vision only when he learned that the Albanian rhapsodes would accept no form of reward. Please God, that had only been a suspicion!

"Did you want to say something to me?" Daisy whispered.

He looked her in the eye for a long moment. He would have to be quite mad to tell her what was in his mind, her especially, the first lady of N——.

He talked about his concerns to Max as soon as they were in the car on the way back to the inn. It was a safe bet that the governor's other guests, as they walked home, were having a good gossip about the foreigners, calling them antisocial, uncivilized, pretentious, or just plain mad.

While he spoke, Bill could not take his eyes off a solitary light blinking in the distance, which only underscored the atmosphere of fright and doom that the black night aroused.

He waited for Max to answer. But Max was silent. He must have gone to sleep.

8

March 14, Buffalo Inn

WE WERE EXPECTING *the weather to get a bit milder, but suddenly winter has returned with a vengeance.*

Fortunately, the cold has not prevented us from making more recordings. Some of them are rerecordings of the same rhapsode, and that's our main triumph.

Our hypotheses about forgetting are being borne out all the time: none of the rerecordings is identical to the first versions. Sung afresh after a week or more (we have no material with a shorter time span), every ballad already bears the first sign of the process of forgetting.

Does this sign foretell the poem's ultimate disappearance? Is it the germ of the disease that will eventually kill it? Or is it, on the contrary, the serum that will protect the ballad from time's attrition? From what we know, it seems that the last conjecture is nearer to the truth.

So we are getting evidence of what we dimly suspected back in New York:

The loss of material from oral epic has nothing to do with the limits of men's power to memorize.

Forgetting is a constituent part of the laboratory.

Just as in the metabolism of living beings, so in oral poetry, death is what guarantees that life goes on.

The question that we first asked — is the forgetting intentional or accidental? — now seems to us too naive. None of the rhapsodes has answered the question so far; but it was not just that no one answered, every one we asked appeared not to understand the question. It seems to me that both kinds of forgetting are part of the process, but are related to each other in ways that remain a mystery (a providential term in this sort of work!).

I must add that omission is only one side of the coin. The other side, which is closely related, is constituted by additions. Lahuta players add lines as often as they leave lines out.

Then we must tackle an apparently vi-

tal issue: what is the rate of loss by any given measure of time — by ten weeks, by ten years, by two hundred fifty years, by a millennium . . . ?

At first glance you would think that the epic corpus is in a state of partial but progressive decay; but the sheer age of the corpus serves to contradict that view.

We did some simple sums, with results that are flabbergasting:

In the ballad about the betrayal of Muj's wife, the modification of the text in the space of a fortnight came to about one thousandth part of the total. At that rate, at the end of two thousand weeks, that is to say forty-odd years, the epic should have disaggregated entirely. But that is far from being the case.

So what has happened?

We scratched our heads long and hard over that problem and came to the conclusion that the greater part of the omissions and additions are no such thing and that they should be renamed pseudo-omissions *and* pseudo-additions.

In other words, most of the apparently new lines are nothing but previous omissions that the bard has decided to restore, just as the omissions concern temporary additions that the bard, for reasons that he is not necessarily aware of himself, decides to clear away from his text. And so on, ad infinitum.

When we have collected dozens and dozens more recordings, then maybe we will be in a better position to elucidate this strange commerce between memory and forgetting. More material would enable us to distinguish the genuine omissions and additions from those that only seem so.

But even that method is not foolproof. How are we going to know why and by what mysterious means a line that has been forgotten and shrouded in darkness for years may reemerge into the light once again? And that's leaving aside the fact that the phenomenon does not just occur within the repertoire of an individual rhapsode but, as if carried along by a subterranean stream, an omitted line can be restored by some other rhapsode, in a different time and place. Epic fragments seem able to climb out of the grave where the bard's body has been rotting away for years, claw their way through the earth, and come alive in another's song, as if death had not changed them one bit.

Mid-March, at the Inn

Brief notes on the role of the ear in oral poetry; eye-ear relations; Majekrah (wing tip):

The German Albanologists who first de-scribed the ancient gesture of majekrah *(and published a sketch of it) advanced the idea that it may just be a response to a physiological need. Nothing more.*

We believe that one has to go into this more deeply. When we asked the innkeeper what meaning the gesture had for him, whether for instance it was related to some ancient ritual or had a symbolic significance, he gave only the vaguest answer, more or less along the lines of the Germans' explanation. Apparently the rhapsodes need to shut off one ear while singing: it has something to do with the modulation of their chanting voice, which resonates not in the thorax but in the head; and also to do with their need to keep their balance, to prevent the chanting from making them dizzy.

"You can't imagine how difficult it is to sing the epic ballads," the innkeeper said. "Long ago I tried it myself, but I got no-where. It makes thunder inside your head, like the sound of an avalanche. If you are not used to it, you could go out of your mind."

There is no doubt that oral epic is primarily an art of the ear. The eye that allows us to understand the literature of today played no great role in the Homeric period. It could even become an obstacle. It is no coincidence that Homer is imagined as a man deprived of sight.

In fact, the rhapsodes are mostly poor-sighted. It's a foregone conclusion that they all feel a degree of scorn for their eyes. Maybe they let their sight deteriorate in a secret manner that only they possess? (Isn't it said that Democritus blinded himself because his eyes interfered with total concentration on his thoughts?)

But imagining the rhapsodes as blind men is maybe only an act of faith, proof of the need to put a distance between art and the everyday world. Blindness, or at least poor sight, is an integral part of the machinery that produces epic poetry. After all, aren't the blind supposed to have memories that are different from those of the sighted?

These are rather attractive ideas, but first of all we should establish whether today's lahuta *players really are poor-sighted or not. We can easily make up some sight-test cards like those used by opticians.*

March 21, Buffalo Inn

Wonderful! We've done a sequence of recordings, some of them repeats.

We've decided to look at the system of oral

transmission, that is to say how one rhapsode borrows material from another and how the borrowed material influences the repertoire. To do that we need to establish a corpus of recordings that would allow us to compare, let us say, the ballad chanted by rhapsode A with the version of the same ballad as performed by rhapsode B who did not usually recite that ballad but picked it up from listening to A's performance.

No easy task. Especially since lahuta *players are such awkward and unbending people.*

The diffusion of oral ballads must follow rules of its own, rules that are quite different from the way things get published nowadays. However, oral diffusion must presumably also have its equivalent of overnight hits, failures, and best-sellers.

But that's only a first step. Finding out what are the changes in a ballad as it passes from one rhapsode to another is not enough. We must also try to find out what happens when the ballad is passed on from one generation of singers to the next. And what happens when the song is transmitted from one period to another, or even over the abyss separating two different eras. And what happens after that.

But there's still more. Since the epics

*exist in two different languages, the problems
are even more inextricable. The bilingualism
of these epic poems makes every one of
the issues concerning them infinitely more
difficult, and we have no clue at the moment
to how to cope with this aspect of
the subject. These epics seem to constitute
the only art form in the world that exists,
so to speak, in duplicate. But to say they
are bilingual or duplicate is to underestimate
the acuteness of the problem: they exist
in the languages of two nations that are
enemies. And both sides, the Serbs and the
Albanians, use the epic in exactly the same
way, as a weapon in a tragic duel that is
unique.*

*A ballad in one of the two languages is
like an upside-down version of the same ballad
in the other language: a magic mirror,
making the hero of the one the antihero of
the other, the black of the one the white of
the other, with all the emotions — bitterness,
joy, victory, defeat — inverted to the very
end.*

*It would be childish to imagine that each
of these nations invented epic poetry independently.
One of them must be the originator
and the other the borrower. We are
personally convinced that, as they are the
most ancient inhabitants of the peninsula, the*

Albanians must have been the originators of oral epic. (The fact that their versions are much closer to Homeric models tends to confirm this view.) But we will not get ourselves involved in this polemic, or in anything that takes us away from our main aim, which is to lay bare the techniques of Homeric poetry. We will deal with the duplication only insofar as it relates to the mechanisms of forgetting, with the formulation of variants, and with the processes of transmission — and no further.

Max has stuck a strip of paper over the mantelpiece saying: WE ARE HOMERIC SCHOLARS FIRST AND FOREMOST.

March, at the Inn

The transformation of a real-life event into an epic — "Homerization":

That's a topic we keep coming back to. It raises many issues. For instance, what criteria determined the choice of events to be turned into epic material? How did the embalming process begin, so as to start turning an event into an immortal story? What are the soft parts — the details and incidents — that got stripped away, and what ancient formulae and poetical models played the role of the embalming fluid?

In order to compare a real event with its Homerized version, we looked for the most recent event we could find that had been turned into ballad material. All we found were twelve lines, no more, referring to the Congress of Berlin of 1878. Like some cold-weather hydra staying hidden in the fog, not daring to come any closer to our times, epic poetry seems to have stopped in that year. Why 1878? What prevented its moving forward? What has frightened it off?

It seems that oral epic had long been wary of approaching the shores of the modern world, which is so foreign to it.

We compiled a very detailed file on the Berlin Congress: the agenda, the statements of the participating governments, the attitude of the Great Powers to the Ottoman Empire and to Albania, the decisions taken; and we even made notes on the maneuvers behind the scenes. The real events seem like a still-warm corpse beside the mummified version the ballad gives.

We are looking without success for a more recent event. We are astonished to find barely a line in the oral epics about 1913, the black year of Albania's dismemberment, a year that ought to echo through the whole of the rhapsodes' corpus! Which suggests very firmly that the art of oral epic has indeed become arthritic with age.

March, at the Inn

What shifts and what stays fixed in epic poetry? Is there an unchanging core of material that ensures the integrity of the art form over the centuries?

Up to now we believed that the anchoring role was played by the figures of speech, the models or fixed forms of the language, or, to put it another way, the basic molds into which epic material was poured.

So we were convinced that the ancient laboratory's linguistic equipment, which was itself unchanging, guaranteed the homogeneity of its poetic production.

However, the more we progress with our research, the more we come to see that, like the laboratory itself, figures of speech and linguistic formulae are also subject to change. Except that the rate of change is so slow as to be imperceptible, just like our own aging.

9

BILL AND MAX FELT EXHAUSTED by the superhuman perspectives that their research sometimes opened up, and so they came back to simpler and more concrete issues, such as the potential influence of a rhapsode's personal life on the omissions or additions that he made to his ballads. If a *lahuta* player stressed the jealousy motif in the rape of Muj's wife, for instance, then the explanation was to be found hidden in the player's own soul. It would have been marvelous to be able to conduct a fully detailed investigation of that kind, but it was a lost hope since, as they had come to realize full well, highlanders would not allow any questions about their private lives. How wonderful it would have been to clarify everything! To elucidate a passage where, for instance, a bridal procession is caught in ice as it crosses the mountains, it would have been desirable to have the details of the rhapsode's own wedding, of the dangers encountered, of whatever worries he had experienced, and so on. Comparing all such information provided by different rhapsodes would have allowed the scholars to establish particularly valuable criteria for measuring the "tragic quotient" of each version.

As the days went by, they began to notice strange correspondences between the epics and memories of their own lives. Half joking, half serious, they started talking about everyday episodes from their respective pasts. Some had taken place in their homes in Ireland, others in telephone booths and bars in New York, then there was the route the taxi took the day Max got married, and his feelings one weekend the previous summer when his wife left a note saying she had gone to see her parents, whereas he suspected her of an affair with an old flame. Bill, for his part, recalled his mother's remarriage, a painful memory that was still torture for him fifteen years after the event. Little by little they hammered out their entire lives on the formidable anvil of the oral epic, and by dusk, they could see the green pastures of the Emerald Isle as well as the skyscrapers of Manhattan against the now familiar backdrop of the Accursed Mountains, on which they had still not set foot.

Had it begun to snow again outside, or was it just an impression caused by his weakening eyes? Bill went closer to the frosted windowpane. It really was snowing. A thin sprinkling of snowflakes. Max was busy with the tape recorder.

Ever since Shtjefen had told them that all sorts of rumors were flying around about their machine, they had tried to keep its volume turned down as low as possible. On one occasion, the screech of the tape rewinding had terrified one of the guests downstairs, who started to scream that a murder was going on upstairs, that someone was being strangled, having his neck wrung.

The innkeeper had tried in vain to calm the man by explaining what the noise actually was. But the man only got angrier.

"So our bards' voices are being put through that torture? Those aren't human voices now, they're the voices of demons! Do you mean to say that you are allowing your inn to be used for such an abomination? Shtjefen, you should be ashamed of yourself!"

As he departed, he yelled out again from the road: "Take care, Shtjefen! You have allowed the devil into your house, do you hear?"

Although the innkeeper told them about only part of this exchange, they were very annoyed. Then, calming down, they persuaded themselves that they could not have expected anything but such disapproval of their work. The publication of part of the corpus of epic poetry some years previously and now their recording heralded the rhapsodes' imminent disappearance. They were becoming increasingly dispensable, and soon, as the days went by, there would be fewer and fewer ballad-carriers, until finally they would become extinct, just as in everyday life technological progress would soon make street sweepers redundant.

They were discussing this topic (Bill remarking that the expression "ballad-carriers" might sound eloquent but was actually inadequate, since the rhapsodes were much more than mere carriers; their decline had much more to do with the aging and rusting of the entire machinery of oral poetry), when they heard a familiar knock at the door: Shtjefen. Even before they could see that the envelopes in his hand were addressed to them, the diagonal red and blue stripes made their hearts leap with joy at the prospect of receiving news from home.

The mail was indeed for them. So the post office had not forgotten them, it had tracked them down to the end of the earth. They tore the envelopes from the innkeeper's hand and began to open them indiscriminately.

"Look, Max!" said Bill as he pulled some press clippings out of one of the larger envelopes.

"Newspapers!" Max mumbled as he looked over. "Are the stories about us?"

They abandoned the letters for a moment and put their heads together to scan the headlines: IS THIS THE END OF THE HOMERIC ENIGMA? There were pieces from the *New York Times* and the *Washington Post:* A BIZARRE ADVENTURE IN A LAND BELIEVED TO BE THE LAST EXTANT CRADLE OF HOMERIC POETRY. Then clippings from two Boston newspapers, and the *Chicago Tribune.*

"What we're doing is out in the open now," Bill said.

They read it all over several times. Some journalists were appreciative, others were not. One article compared their discreet departure from New York to the way that Don Quixote and Sancho Panza left their village on the morning when their tragicomic adventures began. But it didn't say which of them was the knight and which the squire.

The inn had its own life, and as they paid attention to it only intermittently, when they needed rest from their work, it seemed all the more foreign and impenetrable to them. What went on downstairs was always muffled by whispering and shrouded in mystery. The Albanian high-landers were dour folk, who never talked a lot or laughed out loud. They were rarely seen and always vanished like ghosts at first light.

Martin sometimes told Max and Bill what had been going on. One evening there came a group of men looking as dark as the grave, apparently on someone's trail. A few minutes after the group left, the Royal Police Force turned up — and almost immediately after, the fugitive himself. Who knew what was really going on?

Another day, highlanders from the Black Ravine who were taking a sick man to the hospital turned up and asked to stay the night. When the Irishmen went down for their coffee at dawn the unfortunate man was still there on his stretcher. His face looked like a death mask. They asked what his sickness was, and Martin assured them that it was not a contagious disease.

"They suspect that his shadow has been walled up," he explained. "If that is the case, there will be no point in taking him to Tirana. He won't pull through."

"What do you mean by 'his shadow has been walled up'?" Max asked.

Martin tried to explain. It was a fatal malady. The victim was a stonemason, and during the construction of a *kulla*, or round tower, such as you find in the Albanian uplands, one of his workmates had apparently walled up his shadow, accidentally or on purpose; that is, he had cemented a stone onto a wall exactly where the victim's shadow was falling at that moment. Highland builders usually avoid walling up a shadow, as if it were the devil himself, for they all knew full well that if your shadow is trapped in a wall, then you are also imprisoned by it and must surely die. The man lying on the stretcher was, they said, a novice mason, without much experience.

"So there you are," Martin said. "Whether they meant to or not, they have robbed him of his life. It's a terrible shame. To think he is barely twenty years old!"

The Irishmen looked at each other.

"But maybe that is not what is really wrong with him?" Bill queried. "You said it was only a supposition."

"Of course it is only a supposition. Otherwise why would they bother to carry him to town?"

"A strange business!" Bill exclaimed when the two scholars got back to their room. "Very ancient maladies, or rather, an antique explanation given for a malady . . . It makes your hair stand on end!"

The low rays of the afternoon sun caught the metal case of the tape recorder, which answered with a sinister glint. Bill and Max tried not to look at it, but though they did not admit it to themselves, they knew that the machine was at the root of their anxiety, of the obscure and unfocused worry that was eating at them and that neither death nor logic could explain.

One Saturday, they came back to the inn from their morning stroll to find Martin unsaddling a horse in the yard. He told them that a visitor was waiting inside and wanted to talk to them.

A tall man dressed partly in monk's robes, the visitor had the round and ruddy face of a peasant. With a broad smile that spread across his face, he would have seemed a good-natured fellow had there not been a suspicious sparkle in his eyes. According to Martin, he spoke English, Albanian, and Serbo-Croatian.

"I was just passing by when I heard about you and the work you have thrown yourselves into," he said, smiling first to one and then to the other of the Irishmen. "I must say it is a magnificent project, and I wanted to meet you. I am Serbian myself, from the archdiocese of Peja, a long way away from here. I'm on my way to Shkodër, on business — monastic business!"

"I see," said Max, blankly.

"Yes, and I wanted to tell you," the monk went on, "I've had occasion to collect a few epic poems here and there. To the best of my limited abilities, of course, and only in my spare time. We monks do sometimes take an interest in such things. But obviously we're only amateurs, and there's no question of our wanting to set about it in scholarly fashion. What can you expect of a mere monk on his own? Cut off from the world, totally isolated, that's our lot. . . . To be honest, I've always dreamed of meeting people like you. To be able to discuss the ancient epics. But you must be very busy, your time must be very precious. . . ."

"No, not at all," said Bill. "We would also enjoy chatting with you. We came thousands of miles precisely in order to make contact with people such as yourself."

"And it could turn out to be very helpful," Max added, as he asked the monk to be seated. He now felt he had been wrong to be suspicious. "What can I get for you?"

"Thanks, but this round is mine. Even if I'm not

from these parts exactly, I am a neighbor, I don't live a thousand miles away."

"Peja is in Kosovo, isn't it, over the Yugoslav border?" Bill asked.

"That's correct."

They ordered three glasses of raki. When he brought the drinks Shtjefen looked askance at the visitor. In no time at all, they were having a lively, even a heated conversation, as if they were old friends. As he listened to Bill and Max, the monk nodded with surprise and admiration, exclaiming, "We have all this material on our plates and haven't begun to look at it properly. . . . What miserable ignoramuses we monks are! It's heartbreaking!"

After his second glass of raki, the monk's eyes narrowed and his glance grew more piercing.

"But tell me, are you working exclusively on the Albanian ballads? You must know as well as I do that the epic corpus also exists in another language, Serbo-Croatian."

"Yes indeed," said Max. "Obviously we are aware that the epics exist in both languages. But for the moment we're looking only at the versions one gets here."

"If I may be so bold as to ask, why?"

The Irishmen exchanged rapid glances.

The monk's smile began to twist into a different kind of expression but still would not quite leave his face. They had never seen a smile change into its opposite like that while retaining the hallmark, so to speak, of its origin. Such a paradoxical expression made the monk seem all the more poisonous.

"We're scholars," said Bill, "and we have not the slightest wish to get involved in local . . . shall we say Balkan squabbles."

"Never take sides in arguments," the American consul in Tirana had advised them at the one meeting they had had with him. "In this country, disagreements rapidly escalate into armed conflicts. Especially if what's at stake is the ancestry or the paternity of epic poetry. Both sides treat the question as a fundamental part of the national issue and connect it to ethnic origins, to historic rights over Kosovo, and even to current political alliances."

The consul had shown them a pile of Albanian and Yugoslav newspapers and, with a smile, translated extracts, so as to give them an idea of the style of polemical writing in the Balkans. Once both sides had exhausted their available stock of all imaginable insults, the Serbian press declared that for the greater good of Europe, Albania should be wiped off the map of the continent — and the Albanian papers, which presumably thought the same of Serbia, brought the argument to a conclusion by stating that no dialogue was possible between two peoples whose names derived, on the one hand, from the word for "snake" and, on the other, from the word meaning "eagle."

In the ensuing silence at the inn, Max, though tempted to give his opinion, just stretched his arms out wide and said:

"I hope you understand our position, especially as you are a man of the cloth."

"Of course, of course . . . ," said the monk. In a

flash, he reassembled the fragments of his smile and beamed as he had at the start. He went on in a good-humored way:

"It's of no matter, gentlemen. You have done me a great honor by deigning to exchange a few ideas with a poor ignorant monk. Please, again, pardon me my excitement, if I may use such an expression. But I think you understand me — I am Serbian, and I support my nation's cause. It's unavoidable, especially here in the Balkans. Please don't take my reactions amiss."

"No, of course we don't!" said the two scholars as one man. "That's a perfectly comprehensible attitude, and not just in the Balkans, you know."

There followed a short silence, which palpably needed to be brought to an end.

"If I have understood correctly, you aim to use your study of the oral epics to discover just who Homer was?"

Max nodded.

"Indirectly, you are doing the Albanian epic, and the Albanian people in general, a great honor, aren't you?"

"Definitely."

The monk beamed even more sunnily. His face was now that of a profoundly good and even jovial man.

"I won't hide the fact that I am very envious. I would have liked such an honor for my own people. But what can I do?"

"True enough, there's nothing that can be done," the Irishmen replied.

The monk took a pocket watch from his robe.

"Well, well, how time passes. I must go, gentlemen. I will always be glad to have good news of you."

He hastened away. Bill and Max went back up to their room and watched him through the window. He mounted his horse and rode off at a gallop. From a distance, the horse seemed to be pounding the earth with a heavy and furious hoof.

10

O N SOME DAYS THEY IMAGINED that they had succeeded in mastering the vast continent of Albanian
heroic poetry, that they had encompassed it in its entirety.
But such illusions were quickly dissipated: by the next
day, the firm outlines of the epic would grow blurred,
would shift and once again vanish into thin air; and then
the same thing would happen not just at the outer edges
but in every other part of the poetic mass, including its
core. At such moments it seemed unthinkable that they
could ever really command the subject, any more than
they could control a chaotic nightmare in which characters, events, and catastrophes were forever changing their
shape.

The great epic tradition itself seemed to have
suffered catastrophic damage. Splits and cracks ran right
across it; whole sections had been swept away by the im-
pact. From the rubble, bleeding heroes reemerged, their
faces expressing unspeakable horror.

When did the disaster occur? Had the epic tradition
lost its integrity as a result, or had it always been thus,
a poetic haze awaiting the right conditions for condensation? They struggled with these questions in dozens of
discussions, for they were just as relevant to the origins

of Homeric poetry. If the Greek tradition had similarly been just a quantity of unelaborated poetic material at the start, then Homer's greatness would be all the more apparent, for it would have been he who had succeeded in giving it order and discipline. People were wrong to think that Homer was the lesser poet for not having been the only begetter of his works. In all probability, his standing as a redactor would deserve to be higher than if he had been only a rhapsode.

As they tossed these ideas around, the two scholars tried to put themselves in Homer's position, to imagine themselves working in the same conditions, that is to say without books or file cards or a tape recorder, and to cap it all, without eyesight! Good God, they thought, with none of these tools, how did he manage to collect all the lines of the *Iliad,* or rather of the *proto-Iliad,* which he then transformed into the epic that we now have? How did he do it? No sooner did they feel that they were on their way to the right answer than the solution disappeared over the horizon once again. Their vision of the problem grew now clearer and now hazier, swinging back and forth like a pendulum between the contemporary world and the remotest past, as if they were divers returning to the surface for air before going back down into the deep.

It was all closely bound up with the question of who H. was. A poet of genius or a skillful editor? A conformist, a troublemaker, or an establishment figure? Had he been a kind of publisher of his day, the gossip columnist of Mount Olympus, or had he been a spokesman for officialdom? (Some passages in the *Iliad* sound quite like press releases, after all.) Or was he a leader, and, like any other leader, did he have a whole team of underlings? Or was he not any of these things, was he perhaps not even an individual but an institution? So his name may not have been "Homer" at all but a set of initials, an acronym that should be written HOMER . . .

Some of their ideas made them smile, but that didn't stop them from pressing forward with their hypotheses. However bizarre, ideas like these were the urns in which the ashes of the truth would be found in the end. Homer probably suffered some major physical defect, but rather than blindness, his disability was more likely to have been deafness. Deafness brought on by listening to tens of thousands of hexameters? Actually, deafness suited Homer rather well. Blindness was more suitable for later times, when books had been invented. All the same, statues did usually portray Homer as eyeless. But maybe deafness was simply impossible to represent in marble? Maybe the sculptors had solved the problem by substituting one disability for another? In the last analysis, haven't eyes and ears always been associated with each other as the two most characteristic, visible organs of humankind?

"If we go on like that," Bill joked, "we'll end up poking our own eyes out!"

Max looked at him out of the corner of his eye. It wasn't Bill's words about going down the wrong track that struck him, but his friend's allusion to losing his eyes. Bill's eyesight had been getting steadily worse, and Max had thought of asking the governor, at the first opportunity, to help him find an optician. There weren't any at N——, and they would have to go all the way to Tirana. Recently, Max had done his best to steer their discussions away from any questions relating to Homer's blindness.

They kept coming back to the idea that the epic must have had a different structure before the Catastrophe (they used the term now as if it were a proper name). If there had indeed been some catastrophe, then it must have happened at the time of Albania's battle with the Turks. The clash between Christian Europe and the world of Islam had been more brutal and harsh in Albania than anywhere else. The whole country had been shattered, ruined, destabilized; its epic poetry must have suffered the same fate. Whole sections of it were buried beneath the rubble, and the tradition of recitation was banned. The rhapsodes who bore the knowledge of the verse had to flee to the mountains, and they lost all contact with the rest of the world. In those circumstances, preserving the tradition became difficult, because, like everything that has to go underground, it began to change. So that may have been the explanation for the fragmentation of the epic, for the multiplicity of variants, which made it seem unstable and unmasterable.

They thought that if Homer's version of the *Iliad* had not been written down and subsequently published, then it too could easily have fragmented and then been reassembled later on into a quite different shape. The cycles of condensation and dissolution of this kind of epic poetry must have some resemblance to the cycles of creation, fragmentation, and re-creation of possible worlds from cosmic dust.

More and more, epic poetry seemed to them like a kind of poetic galaxy under the sway of mysterious forces. Maybe there were hidden directives coming from the magnetic center, to which the rhapsodes responded by limiting their own freedom, resisting their desire to change, and holding back their rebelliousness. If you looked at it that way, maybe you could understand why rhapsodes always seemed slightly deranged, with a distant look in their eyes, and sang in an unearthly voice whose timbre could have been perfected only in interstellar space.

On other occasions they told themselves that oral epic could only ever exist in the scattered form in which they found it, and they were betraying and altering their material by trying to put its pieces together. In that way of thinking, oral recitation was less like a poetic entity than a medieval order whose members, the rhapsodes, had converted singing into a ritual and spread it far and wide, as if they had been propagating a gospel or a liturgy. A national testament could only have been thus: for the epic corpus that foretold and lamented in advance the nation's division into two parts obviously constituted the First Commandment of the Albanian people. That was how you could account for this thousand-year-long lamentation, this monotonous wail of foreboding made of the unending repetition of an archaic order.

Their minds were so intensely preoccupied with their studies that their dreams sometimes seemed to be no more than the continuation of their thinking, and what they saw while dreaming was hardly different from what they thought about during their waking hours of reading and listening to the tapes. The lack of distinction between waking and dreaming was very much in the spirit of the epics themselves. Space and time obeyed their own fantastical laws in epic poetry: action was spread out over hundreds of years, characters died or were plunged into deep sleep by a spell and then woke, half dead and half alive, to take up the fight; they married in the lull between two wars, went to rest for a while in their graves ("Good grief!" Bill exclaimed one day. "It's as if they were going on vacation!"), then rose again to pursue their gloomy destinies, and so on and so forth. It constituted a faithful representation of a millennial conflict that like a whirlwind had swept away everything in its path. For seven hundred years I shall slay thy progeny, Muj had threatened the mother-in-law of his Serbian foe. His own seven sons, all called Omer, had been slaughtered by Rado the Serb, and all seven had been buried in the Accursed Mountains, Bjeshkët e Nemuna.

In epic poetry, time sometimes flew by at the speed of lightning, and everything that had been foretold for the end of the world would happen in a few instants; in other passages, however, time would decelerate sharply, would slow to a snail's pace: a wound would take ten years to heal; a wedding procession would be arrested and frozen in ice, and would thaw out only after time had gone by, before moving on again to the bridegroom's house where, despite an interval of several years, people still waited for the procession to arrive, just as they had on the first day.

They had come across nothing like this special use

of time in any other European epic poetry, not even in the Icelandic sagas.

It was March, but the days were still as short and dark as in February. Waiting impatiently for the weather to improve, the Irishmen feared from time to time that the first warmth of spring would take them away from the climate of the epic — for, as they had come to realize, epic weather was always wintry. It was initially rather astonishing that a Mediterranean country like Albania could have engendered a poetic climate that was all north wind and glistening snow and ice. The entire corpus of the epic seemed to crackle underfoot like an icebound field. But epic cold was generous, for the snow never melted sufficiently to reveal the mud underneath, and it struck the scholars that the climate had been specially invented to allow its characters to hibernate and to reawaken years later. At first they had taken it for granted that epic poetry originating at six thousand feet above sea level would necessarily be set in a snow-laden landscape, but as more detailed study of the ballads demonstrated, the characteristic climate of the Albanian epic corresponded to a much higher altitude than that, and it was safe to suppose without risk of error that the action was located in an area situated between twelve and fifteen thousand feet above sea level — halfway between the earth and the heavens.

They had been making more recordings, many of them providing perfect material, and were quite satisfied with their progress. The work was going well. They had succeeded in completing their inventory of instances where the Albanian epics coincided with those of the ancient Greeks. They had identified the equivalents of the House of Atreus and of Ulysses, and beyond that they had found doubles of Circe, Nausicaa, and Medea, as well as figures identical to the Furies and the Eumenides, whom the Albanians called Ora and Zana. They had undertaken further research on the question of forgetting by looking at details such as the rhapsodes' diet, including their consumption of phosphorus. (Oddly enough, it turned out that the highlanders' diet contained virtually no fish and even less of the minerals, such as phosphorus compounds, that are believed to improve the memory. Any rhapsode offered such nourishment would doubtless have treated it as a magic potion intended either to intensify memory or to annihilate it.) What's more, they had succeeded in recording a ballad sung by a rhapsode who was thought to have committed a murder the previous week (a "blood debt" paid off), though they failed to establish whether or not this experience had exercised any influence on the poem or its delivery.

Despite all these elements, which complicated their task, Bill and Max felt that they had succeeded in weaving the Albanian epic onto the reels of their tape-recording machine. Each morning when they woke, their eyes turned automatically toward its quietly gleaming lid. They liked to remind themselves that the creation of that device was like a miracle. It seemed to have been decreed that the solution of the Homeric enigma had had to wait until tape recorders had been invented.

Thinking such thoughts bolstered their confidence

and swept away their doubts. They imagined their predecessors in Homeric studies who, after struggling to pierce the mystery as they were doing, had eventually given up, and become ironical, not to say sarcastic, about their original enthusiasm, about their own gullibility, and about anyone who might try the same research again. But the tape recorder was the Irishmen's rampart against failure and ridicule. Earlier scholars, they assumed, would have solved the puzzle of H. long since had they had a tape recorder to help them. The Irishmen were lucky to be alive at the right time: the key to success had fallen into their lap, and in the last analysis, they were simply carrying out the imperatives of their own time.

They had a dreadful fright one night when they thought that the machine had broken down. It was very late, and they were playing back a recorded tape. All at once the volume rose, then the voice slowed down and trailed off into a croak that sounded like a man dying of apoplexy. Bill and Max went as white as sheets. They could not have been more agitated had they been watching one of their nearest and dearest suffering a stroke. They panicked, paced up and down, tore their hair out, turned the instruction manual inside out, until Max suddenly thought of checking the batteries. Thank the Lord! they sighed with relief, when they realized that the only thing wrong was that the batteries were dead.

However, the croaking drawl of the failing tape stuck in their minds. That must be how the entire machinery of the oral epic had run down: its present voice only muffled the death rattle that could be heard nonetheless. The machine had produced just twelve lines for

145

the year 1878 and had painfully squeezed out only four or five for 1913, like the last words of a delirious patient. The epic was now comatose. There was not much chance that it would come to in time to mumble a few more words before freezing forever in the silence of death.

One night, they recorded the rumble of thunder over the high mountains, and another night, the howling wind. They thought that these noises would help them to recreate the right atmosphere back in New York, when they would be working on the tapes at home.

Martin told them one day that he had seen the Serbian monk wandering around the area again; but the scholars hardly remembered whom he was talking about.

Before reporting the significant results of the surveillance carried out this day of the cave known as the Screech Owl's Cavern (or the Hermit's Cave, to give it its other name), I should like to remind the governor that in my report of 1 February I referred to a conversation between the two Irishmen and the Serbian monk Dushan, who in the course of a journey to Shkodër stopped for the best part of half a day at the Buffalo Inn. If I am so bold as to remind you, sir, it is because the significance of the dialogue overheard today at the Screech Owl's Cavern will perhaps be easier to grasp if put in the context of the conversation mentioned above. In addition, prior to giving an account of the later conversation, I

146

*should like to forewarn you, sir — and I do
this not for the sake of justifying any failings
on my part, sir, or to cover up any slackness
in my conduct of the surveillance, but solely
out of respect for the truth — I must therefore advise you forthwith, sir, that said conversation was closer to the gabbling of a pair
of lunatics than to a normal discussion, and
that given these circumstances, the governor
will naturally understand the extent of the
difficulty one has in reproducing its tone correctly. I must repeat that I do not wish thereby
to justify in any way. . . .*

"What a terrific fellow!" the governor said to himself as he raised his coffee cup from the circular mark
that it had left, like a seal, on Dull Baxhaja's latest report. "He's the greatest!" Lower down, the spy gave the
governor his formal assurance that he had always been
careful to have his hearing tested, that he had taken the
test required by regulations only a fortnight before, and
that he had official certification that his hearing was
A-1 and 20/20. Furthermore, keen as he was to maintain
his memory in tiptop shape, he observed all appropriate dietary regulations, did not drink alcohol, and even
though he would prefer to eat rather tastier morsels, he
consumed the required weight of fish per week to provide his system with the right amount of phosphorus,
and even went so far as to take the elderberry syrup that
the doctor had prescribed for him three times a day. He
begged the governor to forgive him his second digression,

a liberty taken not at all for the purpose of obtaining a pay raise or promoting his career but solely in order to establish the credibility of this report and to fulfill the task allotted to him, insofar as the slightest doubt that might be raised as to its truthfulness could jeopardize the further conduct of the surveillance of the two suspects.

"Oh, hell!" muttered the governor as he raised the coffee cup again from its second ring mark on the report. He knew full well that even if he studied rhetoric or jurisprudence or any other subject of that ilk for twenty years, he would never be able to write so fluently or with such style.

Right, let's get on with the story, he thought, as if weary with the preamble. In fact, Dull had guessed that the governor's main satisfaction in reading his reports came from his flowery introductions. If the governor allowed himself to feel bored by the preliminaries and wanted to get to the meat of the report, it was only because he planned to go back to the beginning later on and reread the preamble for pleasure.

Dull went on to inform the governor that on 5 March he had observed the Serbian monk Dushan wandering around the inn once again, but to the spy's surprise, the monk did not attempt to contact the foreigners and even seemed to be avoiding them. The monk had done none of the things that Dull had expected him to do — he had neither stopped at the inn to rest for the night, nor had he continued his journey, nor had he gone back on his tracks — and had thus become doubly suspect, requiring even more vigilant surveillance. The monk Dushan, after illogical to-ings and fro-ings in the backyard of the inn, suddenly set off — and, even more amazingly, set off without his horse — in a direction that led one knew not where, in a directionless direction, so to speak, like a man wandering forlornly in a desert. At this point, Dull admitted, he had hesitated for a few minutes: Should he follow his target and thus abandon his area of surveillance? Or should he wait for the monk to return to the inn, which was where Dull had instructions to carry out his mission? At this point the report-writer felt obliged to inform the governor that his hesitation was quite unrelated to any personal concerns, nor was it the expression of any views that he would certainly not allow himself to hold about the regulations and laws of the state. Definitely not! He had hesitated only because some time before, he had attended a surveillance seminar where the main topic of discussion had been whether or not a good spy, when faced with a target moving away from home ground, should come out of his observation post and trail the target or stay put throughout the duration of his posting, in order to protect the security of said post. Unfortunately, no conclusion had been reached and the discussion had been held over to the next seminar, so that, as the governor would now no doubt appreciate, his hesitation had been but the reflection of this controversy, or rather of the fact that it had produced no answer.

"Wow!" the governor cried out, and he made a nail mark in the margin alongside this whole passage.

Dull then told how he had followed the monk over the fields, observing all the correct tailing procedures, and in the end, to his great surprise, he observed the monk entering the Screech Owl's Cavern, or the Hermit's Retreat, as it had more recently been dubbed (the governor was presumably *au fait* with this development), since the hermit Frok had taken up residence there.

It was easy to understand the link, Dull went on, between a foreigner such as this monk from Yugoslavia and the hermit Frok, especially in view of the well-known interest of foreigners in taking up residence in precisely this part of the country. Taking advantage of his knowledge of the terrain, and fortunately aware of the fact that the cave in question possessed a ventilation shaft, Dull had circled around to the back of the hillock in which the cave had been dug and, given his experience in the chimney business, had found it quite easy to take up position inside the shaft, whence he could hear perfectly clearly anything the two suspects said to each other.

At this point the author of the report requested the governor to please pardon him for returning once again, *en passant,* to the issue of the credibility of his report, or in other words to the reliability of his hearing and his recall, etc., etc. Aware that he could well arouse the governor's justifiable irritation by such repetitions, he would nonetheless like to emphasize, just to make doubly sure that the point had not been forgotten, that part of the conversation overhead at the Screech Owl's Cavern, or, to be more exact, the first part of said conversation, was so similar to the incoherent ramblings of a pair of mental defectives that it could easily raise the most unfortunate doubts about the sanity of the overhearer.

The present writer, Dull went on in the third person,

could have used a very simple device to avoid any possible misunderstanding and inconvenience, and that would have been to omit any mention of the first part of this conversation, on grounds of its being devoid of interest, especially as the present author reached the ventilation shaft with a certain delay and could therefore provide only a necessarily incomplete account. That is what he could have done to make things easier for himself, but his professional conscience forbade him to take the easy option. For even though the beginning of the conversation may have been incoherent and insane, as it did indeed appear to be at first sight, or rather at first hearing, even though it resembled paranoid ramblings, etc., one could not avoid asking the question: what if? What if the ramblings were only apparently mad, what if the incoherence was in fact a secret code used by the two suspects for communicating with each other? This possibility had been enough to persuade the author of the present report to put down in black and white as accurately as he could the nonsense overheard.

At the point when he had got into position by the air shaft leading to the cavern, the two suspects (most of the talking was done, however, by Frok) were exchanging hypotheses about where the eye of the world might be found. As far as Dull could understand, they thought (but most especially Frok, who had asserted this explicitly) that the world, that is to say the terrestrial globe, possessed eyes, just like any other living being, eyes that, in his view, were to be found respectively in the Atlantic Ocean, somewhere between Greenland and the North Sea, and in the Central Asian plains. "One of the eyes is

now very much dimmed," the hermit went on, "and th
planet sees poorly through it, but it would be wrong t
think as most people do that the bad eye is the one locate(
in the steppes. In fact, it is the opposite: the weakene(
eye is the one that I have pinned down to the ocean floor
and the healthy eye is the one I have placed in the dusty
plains of Asia. That is how it is, brother. . . ."

It has to be said, Dull added, that although the Serbian monk took little part in this conversation, he did
nothing to contradict the hermit's assertions. Dushan became a little more talkative when Frok began to explain
how he had recently learned to distinguish normal lightning from lightning that the heavens aborted, just like a
pregnant woman miscarrying. Overall there was one mis-
carriage for every seven flashes of lightning, the hermit
said, but there were troubled times when the proportion
of stillborn lightning was much higher.

That was the tenor of the first part of the conversation, Dull reported, saying that he had not managed to
work out whether the monk Dushan already knew the
hermit or this was his first visit to the cave. But the spy
was now going to relate the second part of the conversation, which was in no way comparable to the foregoing,
and begged the governor to forgive him for reproducing
excerpts in direct speech, a form that in his view would
give a more faithful rendering of what was actually said.

"So now he's going to write dialogue!" the governor
exclaimed. "Not what you'd call an uninventive fellow!"

According to Dull's report, the hermit returned to
the question of the eyes of the world, or more exactly
to the weakening of sight in one of the eyes, which was

certainly going to go completely blind, turning the planet into a one-eyed being, and then he went on about what that would mean for life on earth, and also alluded to the future when the remaining eye would go out in its turn, leaving the world completely blind, until the Serbian monk interrupted:

MONK: I guess you know about the two foreigners — they're Irish, I believe — who've been staying at the Buffalo Inn for some time?

HERMIT: I don't want to know about them.

MONK: You're quite right. I feel the same way about them. They are snakes, and poisonous ones at that!

HERMIT: Snakes? Those two? Don't make me laugh!

MONK: To begin with, the pair of them made the same impression on me. They seemed quite laughable. But when I discovered the purpose of their work, my hair stood on end. To call them snakes is short of the mark. They are the very devil, the devil incarnate!

HERMIT: And what is the work they are doing? I've heard say they have some kind of casket with which they wind human voices like string around a drum, so as to unwind it later on.

MONK: Yes, that's the satanic device that they're using to perpetrate their crime quite openly and brazenly, and people just look on and gawk without suspecting the calamity that will come of it. You called it a casket, I would rather call it a coffin, and that's an understatement. It's far, far worse than that. Compared to what that box means, brother Frok, death itself would be sweet.

HERMIT: They say it's a kind of trunk. . . .

MONK: A trunk indeed! If they had brought the plague, or a gallows, or a guillotine, it would have been better than visiting that horror upon us! A trunk, you say? It's a crate from hell, brother Frok! I'd better tell you all about it. . . .

At this point in the report, the spy requested that the governor forgive him for reverting to classical narrative form, for technical reasons upon which he preferred not to expatiate for fear of irritating his esteemed reader beyond reasonable endurance.

Thereupon the monk proceeded to explain to the hermit how and why the two foreigners were maleficent, and why the casket — the device, or tape recorder, as it was called — was truly infernal. "It is a sinister instrument," he told him, "more evil than witches who dry up springs or wither grass. For if the witch may lay waste grass and water, this machine walls up the ancient songs, imprisons them within itself, and you know as well as I do what happens to a song when you wall up its voice. It's like when you wall up a man's shadow. He wilts and dies. That's what happens to him. It doesn't matter to me, I'm only a foreigner here myself, my land and my Serbian songs are far away, in a safe place, but I deplore for your sake what's going on. With this machine these Irishmen will cut limbs from your body. They'll mow down all those old songs that are the joy of life, and without them it will be like being deaf. You'll wake up one fine morning and find yourselves in a desert, and you'll hold your heads in your hands; but meanwhile those devils will have fled far away. They'll have robbed you of everything, and you'll be condemned to deafness for the rest of your lives. Generation upon generation of your descendants will curse you for having been so careless. It's as I say."

Dull went on to report that at first Frok just listened to the monk attentively, but then he began to snort, and you could tell he was getting excited.

"You're making me angry!" he shouted at the monk. "So now tell me what should be done!"

The monk didn't rush to provide an answer to that question. He advised the hermit to think long and hard about the appropriate steps before taking any action. Then he told him quite suddenly that it was getting late, that he was in a hurry, and that he would return some other day to talk again about the whole affair.

The spy concluded his report by noting that as he was returning to the inn, he noticed the monk striding off along the main road into the far distance.

11

THROUGH HALF-CLOSED EYES, Daisy could just about make out a tuft of her husband's grayish hair on the pillow a few inches away. Still only half awake, she thought: It must be Sunday. Every other day of the week she woke up alone, since her husband went to his office early, and it was only on Sundays that he lay in bed as she did every day.

She opened her eyes fully and looked at her husband for a few moments. His sleeping face asked for pity. The radiators must be off, she thought, and she pulled the blankets up over his shoulders. The last traces of the night's warmth had all but vanished from the bedroom. The mist on the windowpanes had broken up into rivulets here and there, another sign that the heat had gone. The winter really did not want to go away this year. Daisy's mind went over futile and sometimes quite meaningless trifles, as it did every morning, before wandering toward the subject of the two Irishmen, whom she had not seen for quite some time. It was thinking of the winter that kept dragging on that had led her by a curious jump to thoughts of the Irish scholars. They had said something about the end of the winter, hadn't they? Ah yes, that warmer weather would perhaps allow them to set off on a trek into the mountains.

To get even farther away from me! she said inwardly, with a touch of bitterness that was no more consistent than the condensation on the windowpanes. She had never imagined (it's hard to tell why, but even though it was Bill who was mainly in her mind, she always thought of them now as a pair and called them "they"), no, it had never even crossed her mind that they might prove so uninterested in her. But she wasn't offended. She was convinced that it was not true indifference but a side effect of their absence, along with the practical difficulties they would have had if they had tried to come and visit more often. They're so caught up in this Homer business, she thought sourly. She was not far short of feeling outright hostility for all that ancient rubbish.

All the same, she was sure that the Irishmen talked about her. Last time especially, when she was dancing with Bill and he made eyes at her a couple of times, his colleague had offered some remarks and Bill had answered back over her shoulder. Yes, she was sure they had been talking about her. . . .

My lord, my love . . . Daisy heaved a great sigh as she recalled the only words of English that she had learned from the cinema screen. The mere thought that somewhere in the middle of the icy plain, in a godforsaken inn, two men were talking about her in English would have elevated her to a plane of ecstasy.

Another ball will be arranged, then a farewell party, she thought, with melancholy. She would indulge in more reveries, would spend more sleepless nights, and then be crushed by disappointment. Her husband and she would do better to forget the receptions. Why walk into turmoil like that again? Why? she moaned, with tears in her eyes.

But a few moments later, there she was with them again, at a dinner being held in their honor. All the guests from the previous receptions were there, and the fire was burning in the hearth, as it always did. The only difference was that people's conversation had changed mouths, just as you change guests' places at table. Bill was saying what the postmaster ought to have said, and similar permutations had occurred among the other diners, so that Daisy herself — how flattering! — found herself speaking the words of the soapmaker's wife. . . .

The bedside telephone rang and woke her from her dream. She buried her head in the top of the blanket; the heaving of the bed told her that her husband had reached out an arm in his sleep to take the call.

"Hullo," he said in a sleepy drawl. "Hullo, who is calling?"

Even before his voice changed tone, she could feel his body stiffen as if it had been electrified.

"At your service, sir. I am all yours, Minister," he blurted out. "Ah, you got it, did you? Delighted, sir. Excuse me? You have authorized the dispatch of an English-speaking informer? Excellent news, sir. To be honest, I had given up hoping. No, no, don't worry, Minister. We'll catch our chickens in the roost. In double-quick time too — I'll vouch for that, Minister."

During the conversation, Daisy raised the blanket and listened. Who was this English-speaking informer?

she wondered confusedly. Her husband went on talking to the minister. He came out with "catch them in the roost" and "chickens" again.

When he put the receiver down, his face, looking like a vessel filled to the brim, overflowed with a smile.

"Who is this English-speaking informer?" she asked.

"Oh, so you're awake?" he answered gaily. "Obviously, you couldn't not be awake. Damned telephone!"

"You were talking about an informer who can speak English . . . ," she repeated.

"It's administration business. You know what a bore all that is."

"Is it about the two Irishmen?"

"What? Hey, why did you think of them? It's true that . . . Look, Daisy, why don't you go back to sleep and stop tiring your brain with such nonsense?"

"Are you going to have them watched?"

She felt him tense up in bed. Then the springs of the mattress creaked, as if they had relaxed.

"And what if we did? Let's suppose we did what you just said. Would that be the end of the world?"

She clenched her teeth. There was a bitter taste in her mouth.

"That would not be decent. We invite them to dinner, and then . . ."

"Ho ho!" He burst out laughing. "Will you never grow up?"

He stretched out an arm to stroke her face, but she turned her head away in disgust.

"All the same, I love you the way you are."

"Stop bothering me," she riposted, "and let me sleep."

She really did seem to go back to sleep, and after waiting for a moment, the governor got out of bed and slipped from the room as noiselessly as he could. He must have gone to his office to telephone his spies, Daisy thought. She imagined bells ringing in bug-ridden bedrooms, then the bleary-eyed, drink-bloated defectives who called themselves spies reaching for receivers just as her husband had done a few minutes before.

I am the wife of a common petty official, she thought. She had poured out her bile to the prison warden's wife and the wife of the soap manufacturer with no effect. Her husband did dirtier work than theirs, he really did. She was the one to pity, she really was.

She opened her eyes wide. The droplets of condensation on the windowpane reminded her of tears on a tragicomic mask. They're going to listen in on their conversations, she thought with sudden fright. And the Irishmen were so absentminded that they would fall right into the trap. "The chickens . . ." It was not right to call them that. They were totally lost, as if they had been "let drop" by a bird of prey, as Daisy's grandma Mara used to say. Not to mention that those spies would also eavesdrop on the Irishmen's remarks about her. Her own name overheard by mud-filled ears! She tossed and turned in her bed. "I have to do something," she said to herself. This was no time for daydreaming, like at the movies; it was time to take real action. To warn them . . .

She imagined a carriage with curtains drawn setting

off behind a pair of horses. Inside, a woman wearing a black veil, who would be herself. Oh, Lord, she had seen that a hundred times at the movies. . . . But the carriage conveying the worried woman kept on rolling toward the Inn of the Bone of the Buffalo.

The English-speaking spy arrived at N—— at the end of the week. Apart from the governor and one of his staff, no one was aware of the real trade of the black-suited gentleman with the handlebar mustache who took a room at the Globe Hotel. It was natural that inquisitive townsfolk should seek to discover the real reason for the presence of this visitor from the capital, beginning at the very moment of his arrival, and as the information they picked up was not sufficient to satisfy their curiosity, it was even more natural that their inquisitiveness should intensify throughout the following week. It was variously reported that he was a collector of antiques and ancient manuscripts, a beekeeper, and a psychopath who benefited from mountain air. Other hypotheses that would have accounted more or less satisfactorily for the visitor's frequent absences from the hotel might well have done the rounds had a tiny part of the truth not come to light. Did the suspicion first emerge among the town's informers, for entirely comprehensible reasons (relations between colleagues, professional rivalries, and so on)? Or did the spies pick up the rumor somewhere and then, for the same reasons as before, adopt the story for themselves? It's hard to say. But the spies' own interest in getting to the bottom of it is easy to explain. As in all closed circles, in the world of shadows and muffled whispers that was the informers' community, there were stars and there were black sheep, beginners full of admiration for their mentors as well as emotions of jealousy and hatred; there were tyros dreaming of future glory, along with legends about the exploits and adventures of Tirana spies, and lamentations on the difficulties of working in the provinces, and so on. All these tensions were suddenly reenlivened by the arrival of that confident man of the world with oiled hair and handlebar mustache who sauntered infrequently into the dining room of the Globe Hotel.

The most surprising thing was that the rumors circulating in the closed society of the informers ended up leaking out into the wider world. It had been an open secret for years, of course, that the loyalty and commitment of the spies at N—— fell some way short of absolute; indeed, it had been a well-known fact ever since the declaration of the monarchy and the founding of what was then a new profession in N—— by the unforgettable Palok Veshi ("The Ear"), whose real name was actually Gjoku (it had been changed for obvious reasons). But for things to reach such a scandalous pass — in other words, for a rumor to escape from the magic circle of the spies' own community and to resurface in the population at large — well, that really was the limit!

The governor went over the case at great length in discussions with his subordinates and came to the conclusion that the leaking of the secret was not in this case, as it would have been in ordinary circumstances, the result of someone's unavowed wish to forewarn the suspects so as to help them keep out of danger. In his judgment, what confronted him was a phenomenon of a diametrically opposite kind, which is to say that the leak, far from being prompted by compassion for the two foreigners, was in all probability the result of a surge of patriotism among the inhabitants of N— who had received the spy from Tirana with great enthusiasm. (So you think you can step right in with your fat cigars and your funny machines and do whatever you want in these parts? Well, Mr. Foreigner, you'd better think again! You can't even begin to imagine what we're going to do to you, Mr. Foreigner, sir! We're going to get to the bottom of all your little plans and even of your English!) That's what seemed to be the real reason for the leak.

This analysis of the rumor's origin (a resurgence of the patriotic ardor that had admittedly been somewhat muted in recent years in N—) put the governor's mind at rest, so he promptly turned a deaf ear to the further circulation of the news.

Meanwhile the rumor kept on spreading. Even the new spy's real name was now on the lips of the local gossips. There was mention of his special services to the king in Tirana, of his sentimental involvements with society ladies in the capital, including the wives of ambassadors, and much else besides. He was a spy of the very first rank, you couldn't deny it, the local underlings admitted with envy; he was accustomed to working in the vaults of palaces and cathedrals, not in bug-ridden, dung-filled barns, as they were. Dull Baxhaja, who had occasion to crouch alongside the man from the capital in the roof space of the Buffalo Inn, must be feeling quite diminished. But it would actually be a great honor for him to be allowed to work alongside such a star. Unless Dull had been considered unnecessary now and had been moved off the Irish job? Yes, sure, he must have been taken off the job. What use would he be now that the maestro was there?

According to another rumor, however, Dull was carrying on with his surveillance of the foreigners. It was only common sense: even the man from Tirana couldn't stay up in the rafters twenty-four hours a day, and in any case that wasn't even essential. He listened only at quite specific times, and at night he would go back to his comfortable hotel bedroom, leaving Dull in the attic.

One day, Daisy said to her husband:

"I heard about the arrival of a spy who speaks English, but you said nothing about it to me!"

"So what? It's not as if it were important news!"

She carefully watched her husband's eyes shifting desperately around the sitting room, seeking something to look at.

"Thank you at least for not trying to deny it this time."

"Eh?" he said, as he left the room, still pretending to be hunting for something he had lost.

Daisy sank into an armchair and stared at the carpet. From time to time she was overcome by a particular kind of sadness, a slow-moving sadness like a slab of melting snow, more bearable than the pangs of real, acute melancholy. She had not made up her mind to go all the way to the inn. She had dithered and backed off, not seeing how to overcome some of the obstacles, such as whom to choose to accompany her and what explanation to invent for her visit. Sometimes she calmed herself down by saying that what had to happen had happened, that the eavesdropping had been put in place and she could be of no further use to the foreigners, but the opposite thought immediately followed: maybe they had not yet said anything compromising, maybe the disaster could still be stayed. And so the temptation to dash out to the inn would come to the fore again, and she would work out the words she would say to her only real friend, the postmaster's wife, to explain why she had gone to the inn, and then she would once more fall prey to doubts and hesitations: How much of the truth should she tell? And just what would she say exactly? . . .

This is utter torture, she would groan inwardly from time to time. She had never thought she would be so incapable of making a decision. Yet she had to act at once! If she could only manage to tell the Irishmen not to talk about her, so that the filthy ears of the eavesdroppers would at least not hear her name! Maybe they would take the hint and understand all the rest?

The skies were still overcast, but March had nonetheless changed the quality of the light and widened the expanse of the heavens. Bill stood at the window and looked outside, while Max was busy with the tape recorder behind him. The rhapsode's monotonous chant made him sleepy.

Bill was startled out of his daydream by the noise of a carriage in the courtyard of the inn. He leaned closer to the windowpane, wiped off the condensation, but still could not make out who it was walking back to the carriage. For a second he thought he recognized the silhouette, but the form blurred into vagueness once again.

Who is that woman? he wondered. I think I've seen her somewhere before. . . . He rubbed the glass pane with his hand and then shuddered from head to toe as he realized that the haze belonged not to the image itself but to his own vision of it. Were his eyes now so weak as to prevent his making out a person only a few yards away?

He had been increasingly concerned about his eyesight for some time. "Galloping glaucoma," he mumbled, diagnosing the malady that had recently become his living nightmare. He closed his eyes, then immediately opened them, hoping that he had suffered only a momentary loss of vision and he would now be able to see the woman getting into the horse-drawn carriage. But it was as before, and everything, even the carriage, seemed to have been swallowed up by fog.

"Max," he said, turning around to speak to his friend. "We must go to Tirana right away. I can hardly see anything anymore."

The governor could hardly believe his eyes when he slit open the envelope. Instead of Dull's daily report, it contained a letter of resignation.

"Have I gone mad or has Dull?" he cried out. "Resigning just when the affair of the two foreigners is about to bear fruit?"

To the governor's amazement, the informer began his letter by begging to be excused for causing such trouble, but once he had read the submission, the governor would probably think that either he himsel had lost his marbles or it was the present writer, Dull who had gone off his rocker.

But no, the spy went on, it was not so: the governor was not hallucinating, and he, Dull, had not gone mad. He was in full possession of his mental and physical faculties, and he was asking to be relieved of his responsibilities.

Malicious persons, he continued, would no doubt attempt to explain this request as a petty maneuver related to dissatisfaction over his rank, for instance, or his salary, etc., but he trusted that the governor knew Dull well enough to believe that he had never allowed ambition or personal interests to influence his work. People of ill will would perhaps attribute his resignation to the humiliation, or even the jealousy he had allegedly experienced on the arrival of the English-speaking spy. Coming from them, such an explanation was entirely natural, since just as a cucumber is nine-tenths water, so their lives consisted in equal proportion of offenses suffered and resentments harbored.

Nine-tenths water! the governor repeated to himself. Dull knew so many things! More than a mere spy, that man had the makings of a university professor, he thought.

That's what such sorts might think, the spy wrote, whereas the governor himself certainly remembered that it was he, Dull, who had clamored, perhaps to the point of irritating the governor, for the detachment to N—— of his colleague from the capital.

No, he concluded, absolutely no part of what was going to be said about him would be true. And to make a long story short, he would now lay out with as much clarity and honesty as he could the real reason for his resignation: on 11 March, at 11:00 A.M. precisely, after seven years of true and loyal service to the kingdom as an informer, he had for the first time nodded off while on duty.

Oh, so that's it. The governor sighed with relief. It was an open secret that most officials in N—— took a nap during working hours, especially during the summer. But Dull wanted to be different. And to make his confession look all the more tragic, the spy had framed it in thick black lines, as if it were a bereavement card.

Nobody had seen him, Dull went on, so he could have confessed nothing, seeing that he was at that time alone in the attic of the Buffalo Inn. He could have kept quiet about it, but he didn't have it in him to cheat. He had never hidden anything from the state. With only his own conscience to keep watch over him, over the years he had undertaken all the exercises that a good spy should practice on his own, such as training his ear in difficult, not to say extremely hard acoustic conditions — against the howling wind, the pelting rain, the rumble of thunder, the sound of the sea, dogs barking, crows crowing, owls hooting, and so on. He had never allowed himself to be overcome by sleep, neither in sultry summer heat nor in winter's icy blast; he had kept awake forty-eight hours at a stretch and even resisted, as he crouched in attics, the snoring of his dozing suspects below. In addition, he had always reported in writing everything he had heard and seen, without adding or omitting anything at all, without having recourse to any tricks or wheezes. He had accomplished his task in secret and in silence, as is the lot of every spy; he had made every effort not to breathe a word of it to anyone and to remain unseen, and on the other hand to be as open and frank to the state as was imaginable. For which reason he could not hide what had happened to him on that morning of March 11.

The governor sighed deeply before reading on.

On March 11, at 11:00 A.M., the informer related, while lying as per usual above the ceiling of the room at the Buffalo Inn where the two Irishmen had been listening for some time to a recording of a rhapsode, he had suddenly become aware of the rumble of a carriage in the backyard of the inn. What carriage is this? he asked himself straightaway. Where has it come from? Why had he not heard it coming sooner? He rubbed his eyes, thinking he must have been drowsing for a second. Drowsing, indeed! To his great shame, he had actually fallen asleep! To such an extent that when he had been wakened by the noise of the carriage, he had not had all his wits about him and so he only half saw a woman as through a thick fog getting into the carriage and speeding off.

There was no point going on at any length about the shock he had suffered. It was not simply that he had failed to recognize the woman, not merely that he had missed the conversation she might have had with the suspects. In fact, it was impossible to tell whether she had actually met them. As for her identity, that would presumably come to light later on. But those were not the real reasons for his upset; far from it. The catastrophe had happened inside himself: it made him feel like a cracked vase, shattered from top to bottom. Suffering intolerable pain, consumed with howling remorse, he had fallen into a state of irremediable despair. He would ask for neither pardon nor comfort. Words of consolation would simply exacerbate his torment. He asked one thing only: the right to retire to a life of oblivion. Which was why he was submitting to the governor, in accordance with all necessary regulations, his official request to be relieved of his functions as informer to the kingdom.

The governor gazed for a long while at the signature that he had got to know so well. He felt a wave of sorrow and, simultaneously, acute irritation. What sense did this abrupt resignation make? Was it really conscience-stricken remorse, or was it a cover for something else?

Dark and turgid thoughts, heaped one upon the other like rain clouds, floated through his mind. Who could the woman be? Alongside the sadness he experienced at the prospect of life without Dull's reports — a sharp pang of regret, with a vague touch of nostalgia for his lost youth, as if this episode were the end of an era — he also felt suspicions: had Dull really not recognized the woman, or was he behaving this way so as not to have to give her away?

The governor's head was throbbing, an aftermath, it seemed, of an odd spell. "Retire to a life of oblivion," he said aloud, repeating Dull's words. He would bet that Dull wasn't going to vanish from circulation, except in order to reappear later as a mysterious visitor, or a prophet, or even as a claimant to the throne! God knows, with a man like that, you could not rule anything out! It sometimes occurred to him that his favorite spy had the potential to rise to inaccessible heights, to the very stratosphere, to the rank of chief spy to the terrestrial globe!

That last thought brought a shiver to his spine. He could feel his mind going over the brink, but he was unable to stop himself. The hermit's ramblings about the eye of the world somewhere in the Central Asian plain had had their effect. . . .

He suddenly realized that he had never actually seen Dull Baxhaja, "The Eaves." Year after year, he had read his reports without having the slightest notion of the man's appearance or his voice. Without ever having seen or heard him! And in the whirl of his mind he almost shouted, "Does he really exist?"

He stood up from his chair sharply to put a stop to this latest wave of dementia.

12

*E*ACH DROP OF THE LIQUID made the blank stare of the pupil seem even more pitiable. The first drop, then the second, then the third clouded the pupil beneath a glaucous film.

After four days' treatment with a new and powerful medicine that had only just come onto the market and which they had been amazed to find available in a Tirana pharmacy (apparently the queen mother, who had problems with her eyes too, had ordered it from abroad), Bill had the feeling that his eyesight was improving slightly.

As a result, the scholars' morale, which had been badly dented by Bill's state of health, took a turn for the better. The gradual lifting of the winter weather contributed to their spirits. That very morning, Bill had been full of good cheer and had shouted out:

"Hey, Max, do you see that bird? It's flying toward the Accursed Mountains, isn't it?"

Max turned his head toward the window.

"That's where it's heading, all right. It's a miracle, Bill."

Bill was perfectly aware of the double meaning of

these words. It was a miracle that he had managed to make out a bird in flight and, what's more, tell where it was flying. Also miraculous was that the flight of the bird confirmed the advent of spring. For most of the year, no birds overflew the Accursed Mountains; that was one of the reasons for the mountains' name.

"A holy miracle, Bill!" Max emphasized, clapping his hands.

Bill's sickness had ruled out their planned trek into the hills for some time, but now it seemed that it could come back onto the agenda. They even asked Shtjefen to hire a carriage for them and to permit Martin to accompany them, if they undertook the expedition.

The trip into the mountains would be the crowning event of their project. They now knew exactly where to find the usual dwellings of eleven rhapsodes, whom they would record, some of them for the second and others for the third time.

Furthermore, they had not abandoned a faint hope, against all reason, that they would stumble upon the very last stammerings of the epic machine — that is, lines of verse dealing with some event later than 1913. Since the epic had produced twelve lines for the year 1878 and, thirty-five years later, another five lines for 1913, surely it was possible that twenty years further on it could have secreted another two or three? In fact, given the antiquity of the epic, these decades that seemed so long to contemporaries were just crumbs of time, a few minutes more or less in the time scale of tradition.

They were perfectly aware that their hope was without foundation. The epic awoke from its long slumber in

1913, that was true, but only because a terrible calamity — the dismemberment of the country — had prodded it into a final burst of life. The following period of Albanian history had been utterly uneventful. There was perhaps no imaginable period more appropriate for the final death of oral epic.

Max and Bill had gone over this in discussion, but they realized with some surprise that, for all that, they had not stopped hoping to find an *epivent,* the word they had coined for a contemporary event transformed into epic verse.

Whereas they had previously despaired at the dispersion of the Albanian epic tradition, they now felt reassured that the entire corpus was in good order. What had seemed, to begin with, like shards scattered through space and time, as ungraspable as a mane of rainbows, as wind and burnt dust, quite impossible to collect, was now locked in numbered metal reel cases. Sometimes it seemed hard to credit that they had managed to tame all that hatred and all that passion.

Daisy had never watched the path from the front gate to the front door with such concentration. It was raining, and the flagstones gleamed with a strange and disturbing light. She knew the flags intimately, each individual one, and remembered which of them, wobbling slightly, was likely to splash her stockings on rainy days, never forgetting to step around it. But this was the first time that she had studied them from above, from the second-floor window. And on this occasion she could not easily have brought to mind which flagstone might tip and muddy the trouser leg of the man who was on his way.

The English-speaking informer was due to call in a quarter of an hour. A man she did not know calling on her at 11:00 A.M., without her husband's knowledge . . . But the shudder of the illicit lasted only a few seconds. With some bitterness, she went over the scenario in her mind: The man was coming at her invitation, for a quite specific reason, related to his professional responsibilities. She had not found it easy to draft the brief note that said: "I wish to meet you on an important matter. I beseech you, please ensure that this remains strictly confidential."

She had made her resolution a week earlier, after having tried and failed to meet the Irishmen at the Buffalo Inn. The trip in the horse-drawn carriage on the main north road, supposedly to see a fresco at the church of Saint Mary, the stop at the inn, her going in allegedly for a glass of water, the few words she exchanged with the innkeeper, then the return journey in the carriage — all these episodes came back to her in a haze, as if they had not happened at all but were only figments of her daydreams.

Since her attempt to meet the foreigners had unfortunately failed, she had racked her brains for days to find another way of getting a message to them. Another trip by carriage would undoubtedly have aroused the suspicions of the innkeeper; and she did not have the courage to take the postmaster's wife along with her. She had thought of having her maidservant — the one person in the household whom she trusted entirely — take them a short note. While exploring this possibility in her mind, she suddenly thought of the new informer. What if she should speak to him directly? After all, wasn't the English-speaking spy the key to the whole affair, the alpha and omega of the business? It was a bold idea, and an attractive one. There was no doubt about it: the informer was the key to it all. His ear was the direct connection with them. Who else could tell her whether Bill and Max had in fact spoken about her in their magical English? *My lord, my love* . . . Even without admitting it to herself, she was not unaware that the main reason for each of her actions and her final decision to write that note to the spy was her desire to reestablish contact with the Irishmen. Of course, she said to herself in her infrequent moments of lucidity, they are citizens of another country and are not taking any real risks. But she would quickly put that thought aside: most of the time, as now, when she waited for the garden gate to swing open momentarily, she liked to believe that she, Daisy, was saving them both from danger.

It was nearly eleven, and the spy could arrive at any moment.

In her later recollections of the episode, there would be two versions of the man's arrival:

In the first version, the spy came in slowly, and Daisy, watching from the window, followed each of his steps as if the whole thing were happening in slow motion: the gate opening, the steps on the wet flagstones, the ring of the doorbell, his climbing the stairs, then his words: "Madam, I am delighted to be able to be of some use to you."

In the second version, the visitor had seemed to

fly from the garden gate to the second-floor sitting room without touching the ground, until he was there, staring at her with eyes incandescent with curiosity, attraction — and something else, halfway between self-confidence and sheer cheek. Good God, exactly what a spy's eyes should be! she thought. Then the same words: "I am delighted to be able to be of some use to you."

He was exactly as she had expected him to be and at the same time not at all what she had imagined. His oiled, black hair was fearfully shiny, as if made of the same stuff as his eyes. She had never seen anyone with eyes and hair in such perfect accord. A spy's eyes, blended with the glance of a courtier. Judging by the way he studied her face, she reckoned that he had indeed overheard the Irishmen chatting about her. Yes, yes, his eyes were full of tacit messages, of the sort that pass between people who have a shared secret. Her desire to know at once what the foreigners had said was overwhelming. Had she not been a rather timid woman, she would have beseeched the spy there and then: I beg you, tell me quickly, just as you heard it, in English (you can translate it later), tell me everything, absolutely everything, they said about me!

But she had some self-control. She began by beating about the bush. In her later recollection, this part of the conversation would be even more of a muddle than the rest of it. In fact, she wouldn't be able to recall anything very precise about it, apart from the fact that while she was speaking, his eyes sparkled like two burning coals constantly fanned, and that she imagined he knew a great deal more about her than she could guess.

"I know the two foreigners who passed through

here," she said at long last, in a muted voice. "You would be amazed to know the circumstances. . . . All the same . . ."

The spy interrupted in a whisper, as if he was concerned not to wake anyone in the house:

"Madam, I can see that you are embarrassed, but you must realize that I have a great deal of experience in situations of this kind. . . ."

"Of course," Daisy replied, raising her eyes to meet his.

His face was now quite close to hers, and the various stories Daisy had heard about the spy's exploits crossed her mind vaguely. Just as you would expect, she thought, as she smiled limply at the man. Courteously and respectfully, he took her hand in his.

"How beautiful you are!"

"How can you dare to say such a thing!" Daisy's eyes brimmed with outrage.

The spy did not let go of her hand but sought to look straight into her eyes.

"Madam, my professional calling gives me so many opportunities to . . ."

"I know, I know, I've heard all about you and your . . ."

He smiled, and continued in an even more conspiratorial whisper:

". . . so many opportunities to cast my eyes on ladies in bathrooms and bedrooms — society ladies that other men only dream of greeting from a distance. . . . Including you, perhaps, when you visited the capital and stayed at the Continental Hotel . . ."

"Good God!" Daisy screamed inwardly. She had indeed stayed at that hotel. The very thought made part of her brain go numb. What if he had seen her entirely naked? What would that mean? She heard a small voice cry out inside her. If he really had seen her naked, then it would be the same as . . .

He put his head on hers and tasted the perfume of her hair, and Daisy's mind clouded over. She needed something to support her, and yet all her thoughts converged on a single point: if what he said had already happened, then all the rest was just a technicality.

She felt his hands take hold of her by the waist, and instead of pushing him off, as she had intended to right up to that moment, she let herself go.

He's gone, then, Daisy thought as she heard the garden gate screech on its hinges. She slipped a dressing gown over her bare shoulders and went to the window, pulling back the curtain. It was still raining outside, as if nothing had happened. He could at least have told her what the Irishmen had said about her, she mused, as she stood there still dazed. She hadn't managed to ask the question. Besides, she wasn't that interested anymore. Something had entered her whole being, and she didn't want to think about anything else. She stepped slowly toward her bathroom, turned on the hot water tap, and got into the bath.

She was still soaking in the water when her husband came home for lunch.

Shortly after, as she laid the table for the midday meal, the governor reported rumors that were making the rounds about the king getting engaged to a Hungarian countess.

"Is something the matter?" he asked, realizing with surprise that she was not taking any interest in gossip about the royals. "Have you got a headache?"

"Yes," she answered. "I've had a headache all morning."

He bowed his head over his plate, feeling guilty as he always did when Daisy's headaches were mentioned. He was well aware that the main cause of his wife's migraines was the fact that she had never had a child.

Lunch proceeded in that vein, with sparse remarks from the one and the other, then Daisy declared that she was going to lie down for a while. After a short rest, her husband went back to the office.

It was the same routine in the evening, the only difference being that the governor, instead of going back to the office after dinner, shut himself in his study; Daisy, for her part, went back to her bedroom.

She tried to sleep but could not manage it. She was now sure that she would have to face a sleepless night marked by the resonating, lonely chimes of the bronze clock. She could not understand why she had insomnia. It was the first time that she had deceived her husband, but she felt no remorse. No, there was something else, an unbearable emptiness, along with the feeling of having cheapened herself completely. Where did that feeling come from? She could have laughed at herself sourly: of course she knew where it came from! She had been dreaming of something altogether different — of an affair with a foreign Homeric scholar, of his speaking

English, etc., etc. — and she had ended up in the arms of a mere informer. And not just any informer! She had slept with the spy who was eavesdropping on the man of her dreams. Such irony . . .

As if that were not enough, she could already imagine the scene with the bleary-eyed gynecologist, animated by sheer inquisitiveness: "With whom? . . ." No, no, no, she screamed inside herself, she would never tell him the truth. She would make up stories, fabricate a novelette, or an accident (she was a bit tipsy, at a dance, and what's more, it was a complete coincidence that . . .), but she would never let out what had really happened. That thought calmed her somewhat. The throbbing in her forehead eased off. Perhaps I am not pregnant, she thought; and she became quite serene. She hadn't needed to get so worried. In the end, she was neither the first nor the last woman to whom such things happened. Half of the films that were made contained episodes of this kind, and when you think of books — *Anna Karenina, Madame Bovary,* and so many others whose titles she couldn't remember . . . Oh, if only she could go to sleep! Her migraine had subsided in fact, and everything was getting better, apart from her forehead. . . . Where was that cruel noise coming from — a hammer beating time, a thudding bell, quite outside her head? . . . She buried her head under the pillow in the hope that she would manage to muffle the reverberations, and at that moment she felt her husband turning over in bed, as if he had guessed what was going on in his wife's mind. Could he possibly have seen through it all, or was the noise really coming from outside, just to increase her distress? Her skull was still hurting when she heard her husband say:

"Someone's knocking at the door!"

"What!" She sat up with a start; she did not understand what was going on at all.

She saw his arm move and stretch out to switch on the bedside lamp. His voice made an entirely different sound in the illuminated bedroom:

"Someone is knocking at the front door!"

The knocks could now be made out distinctly, and over the rattle, you could hear someone pleading:

"Mr. Governor, sir! Mr. Governor, sir!"

It was *his* voice, she realized with horror. She shook her head from side to side as if to get rid of such an absurd idea. Her husband leaped out of bed and went to the window.

"Mr. Governor, Mr. Governor!" came the cry from outside, but now it was firmer and clearer.

"The English-speaking informer!" the governor said aloud, quite taken aback. "Something must have happened. . . ."

She stared wide-eyed at her husband as he blundered around the bedroom, looking for his shirt, then his trousers, then his jacket.

"No!" she croaked, in a sob that sounded so different from her usual voice that despite his agitation, the governor stopped momentarily and looked hard at her, as if he could not quite believe that the sound had come from her. "Don't go!"

Several possible explanations for their being disturbed like this at such an hour were thundering around in her brain. Good news could not have brought the spy to hammer and yell at the door. My God, she moaned to herself, what can this new misfortune be? Maybe he had gone half crazy and was coming to take her away, to tell her husband about their relationship and to persuade him to let her go, or else he was there to humiliate him, or to mock them both, or simply to kill her husband, or perhaps to apologize. At that point, all these surmises seemed equally plausible, and just as incredible. Perhaps he had repented of what he had done, or worse still, maybe he had had a stupid crisis of conscience and, as the committed servant of the state that she supposed he must be, was on his way to confess to his boss that he had broken a cardinal rule of conduct by revealing state secrets in exchange for a moment of pleasure. . . . But I did not ask him anything, I didn't even get so far as to tell him why I had asked him to come here! she protested to herself, painfully trying to justify herself. All these ideas whirled around in her head as she stared hard at her husband, getting dressed.

"Don't go!" she pleaded a second time.

Containing his own excitement, which was no less acute than his wife's, though of quite a different order, the governor at long last replied:

"Daisy, something has obviously happened, but there is no reason for panic."

She did not have time to ask him a third time not to go out as he was already tumbling down the staircase. It's all over, she thought. There was no way of stopping things now.

She jumped out of bed and went to the window.

She heard the knocker at the door once again, then the voice, now growing hoarse with the shouting: "Mr. Governor, sir! Sir!" She opened the window, and the cold, rain-soaked air chilled her through her nightdress. She could hear her husband's footsteps, and then the metallic screech of the bolts being drawn, which made her spine tingle. She held on to the sill so as not to fall, and listened to the men's voices overlapping each other. She could not make out what they were saying: their words were punctuated by groans and exclamations of anger and indignation.

They drew closer to the front door, and it would hardly have surprised her to hear the shots of dueling pistols. She was still glued to the window, like a trial defendant waiting to hear the guilty verdict. The wooden stairs creaked beneath the men's footsteps. Any minute now and they'll push through the door of this bedroom . . . but they went into the governor's study. She heard the noise of the telephone dial, and then her husband saying: "Hello? Is that the police?"

What! she almost screamed out loud. The police for such a matter? How did they come to an accord so quickly? It was just not possible!

She heard her husband speaking again in his study: "It's urgent — I need ten of your best men, right away!"

Her mind went completely blank. The bedroom door swung open at last, and he stood there stock-still, bewildered at finding the bed empty. Then he must have caught sight of her silhouette at the window, and he said:

"Something awful has happened, and I must leave
at once."

"But what is it? What's happened?"

"Up there, at the inn . . . The Irishmen have been
assaulted."

"Were they killed?"

"No, but they may be hurt. . . . I'm off. Get back in
bed and go to sleep."

He closed the door, and Daisy returned to the window. Though she was shivering from head to toe, she
stayed there until the sound of the men's voices and the
noise of motorcars had faded into the far distance.

"What a crazy night!" She sighed, putting her hand
to her forehead and closing her eyes. Then she muttered
a correction: "As if the day was sane . . ."

When the governor returned, in the small hours, he gave
an extremely vague account of events to his wife. Instead
of casting any light on matters, his words extinguished
the very last glimmer of her understanding.

Twice or three times, she was on the point of asking questions to get him to go over it all again, but he
persuaded her to let him be.

"Don't ask me anything. I really didn't understand
most of what went on myself. It's all such a mess. . . .
Whew! What a mix-up! What a puzzle! I'm going to try
to sleep for an hour or two, to get over it. My head feels
like it's going to burst."

She waited for him to wake, in the hope of getting something more precise out of him, but in vain.
He had become even more sibylline. As if he had taken

his nap solely in order to justify his mental confusion, he appeared quite unable to tell whether the events of his story had really taken place or some of them came from a dream. All he recounted seemed so far from credible that Daisy thought he was trying to pull the wool over her eyes, and she promptly began to speculate that maybe the spy had taken the opportunity during the journey to . . . But she abandoned that suspicion right away when the telephone rang, and the affair, echoing and amplifying along the telephone lines, became ever more substantial and convoluted.

The fact is that later on, when it was full daylight and the first reports reached her, followed by the statements and depositions, and much later, when everything had been written down and properly sorted out in the prosecutor's files, and even when some of the events had been mentioned in the press, things became hardly clearer than they had been in the story the governor told his wife before dawn on that unforgettable day. Daisy suspected that it was actually the same story, simply decorated with a few details.

According to the various reports and eyewitness accounts (the main witness being the English-speaking informer), the affair could be summed up more or less as follows:

Toward two in the morning, the informer, who had been obliged to take over Dull Baxhaja's job after the latter's unjustifiable dereliction of duty and was therefore in the attic, directly above the Irishmen's bedroom, heard first a noise, then a sharp scream. All the other witnesses corroborated the scream, but the explanations given varied widely. The spy declared in his report that he believed the scream to have been recognizably the voice of Martin (which tallied with Martin's having been the first to be injured by the assailants), but others, including Martin himself, claimed the scream had come from someone else.

Some said it was one of the other guests at the hotel; some said it must have been a bandit, yelling out because he had bumped into something, or been hit in the dark by Martin, or, even more simply, just to create an atmosphere of terror before the attack. As for Shtjefen, he thought it was the Irishmen who had shrieked, which would have been the most plausible explanation had Martin not said he was certain that he heard the shout before the bandits broke down the foreigners' door. Some even went so far as to think that the shout had come from the informer himself. . . .

As he leafed through the file, the governor was amazed to see how much significance most of the people present at the inn that night attached to the shout, though in truth it could hardly be considered a major element in explaining the overall facts of the case. He confessed his puzzlement to the witnesses, who stared at him as if he had just committed an unbelievable faux pas, and the governor became ever more firmly convinced that he would never be able to see eye-to-eye with them on that score. He was more and more inclined to believe that no one had actually shouted, and the shout that each of them thought had been uttered by another was only the inner shriek none of them had been able to restrain.

So, hard upon this actual or supposed yell, the front door of the inn was broken down by a gang of persons unknown, whom everyone, in the first moments of mayhem, had taken to be bandits, or murderers, or fugitives from a lunatic asylum. The first to stand up to them was Martin, who got hit on the head with a crowbar. Some of the hotel guests were armed, but none of them managed to use their weapons — because of the dark and the element of surprise, and also for fear of hitting a bystander. The innkeeper succeeded in getting an oil lamp lit, but someone, no doubt one of the bandits, smashed it out of his hands. Nonetheless, in the few moments of light that it gave, the lamp had allowed him to identify the hermit Frok, and that identification was to prove fatal to the assailants. In chaos and confusion, stumbling in the dark over Martin's injured body, they made for the wooden staircase so as to reach the second floor and thus the Irishmen's room, proving that they had come with precisely that intention. As the bandits began to force their door open, the Irishmen started to shout: "What's going on? Who goes there? Help!" The spy was at this moment still up in the attic, and so he heard everything that happened subsequently: the door broken down, the screaming of the intruders and of their victims, groans, curses, and blows delivered to a metallic object. At that point he left his observation post, clambered down by means of the window frame to the backyard of the inn, and rushed into town to make his report.

When the governor and the policemen arrived, they found a nightmarish spectacle. By the light of the sole oil lamp that had remained unbroken, they could make out the traces of the vandals' attack. Apart from Martin, several travelers had been injured, as had one of the Irishmen. The other scholar was weeping, with his head between his hands. All their equipment had been broken beyond repair, especially the tape recorder, which had apparently been the main target of the brigands' fury. Not content just to smash up the machine, they had torn the reels to shreds and thrown cut-up bits of tape all around the room.

It had all taken only a few seconds. But by the time the travelers downstairs had come to their senses, the bandits had already evaporated into the night. According to the innkeeper, at the time when the governor arrived with the police escort, the brigands could not yet be very far away. One of the fugitives had probably been injured when a hotel guest opened fire (everyone had heard the cry of pain), so that the governor, if he cared to take the trouble, could very probably lay hands on part of the gang.

Just as the governor had ordered the policemen to set off on the bandits' trail and capture them before they reached the high mountains, Shtjefen recalled an important detail that he had theretofore failed to give: he had recognized one of the vandals as being Frok.

The manhunt began immediately. Fortunately for the pursuers, there was faint moonlight, so the policemen, driving slowly along the main north road with their van lights extinguished, could make out the bandits' silhouettes from a long way off. The first to be caught were the injured man and the two companions who were helping him along. The others were taken a little farther on, just at the foot of the mountains. As for Frok, he was found in his cave, ranting and raving.

The whole town of N—— was buzzing with the story from dawn the next day. A small crowd gathered in the street in front of the prison, expecting to catch sight of this band of hooligans, whose motives remained a mystery. Despite the drizzle that began to fall, the crowd did not disperse. They hung around until at long last the prisoners appeared at the end of the street, chained together in pairs. Their waxen faces looked even paler under the locks of hair that the rain had glued to their foreheads. Their eyes bulged as if they were ready to pop out of their sockets.

"It's the hermit Frok! It's Frok!" two or three people whispered fearfully as the small procession of prisoners and policemen drew near. "Look at the rascal!"

"Good God, their hands are all bleeding!" an old woman muttered. "People should not be treated like that."

"No, granny, you've got it wrong," someone explained. "That's not blood you can see on their hands, but rainwater dripping off their rusty handcuffs."

The report that appeared two days later in one of the national newspapers began with a description of the men arrested, referring to them variously as bandits, fanatics, and members of a secret sect. The article went on to give a few details of the case and ended with a picture of the smashed machine and reels, alongside a short and completely impenetrable interview with one of the foreign scholars. "Now the epic is scattered again, just as it was before," one of them had declared with tears in his eyes, pointing to the pile of shredded magnetic tape. "We tried to put it all back together, but it has been torn to pieces, just like that . . . as if it had been hit by a natural disaster." The journalist emphasized that the foreign scholar had used the word *catastrophe* several times, qualifying it on one occasion as *cosmic*.

13

THEY BARRICADED THEMSELVES in a room at the Globe Hotel for forty-eight hours and refused to meet anyone. On the third day, they took a dray to the Buffalo Inn to collect their cases. The sky was overcast, and it was as cold as a winter's day. In Martin's absence, Shtjefen helped them carry their bags to the carriage, almost without a word. They left the wreckage of the tape recorder there, since it was no more than a piece of junk, like most of the reels of now unplayable tape. They were tempted to take some of the less damaged reels with them in the hope that something usable would remain, but in the end Bill said:

"No, let's leave them behind. I don't think they'll ever be of any use."

He kept rubbing his eyes, and though he did not complain about it, Max guessed that his friend's sight had suddenly clouded over. As the vial of eye medication had been smashed along with everything else, the course of treatment had been interrupted and Bill's condition had taken a turn for the worse.

They got into the horse-drawn vehicle and turned to take one last look at the door of the inn, whose half-legible sign seemed to cast a shadow of oblivion and abandonment on the surrounding countryside. Every sound and every movement only heightened their feelings of deep bitterness and irreparable loss. They had come close to finding the key to the puzzle of Homer, and just as they were about to grasp it completely it had been torn from their hands, for no reason, for nothing at all! To cheer themselves up, they sometimes said they could always come back next year, or a few years later, and start their research all over again, but they themselves knew it was not true, that they would never come back. For even if they did travel once again to these parts, they would encounter no trace of the rhapsodes, or if they did, they would find only a handful, and they would have gone deaf; and not only the rhapsodes but this whole last laboratory would thenceforth be buried under the ashes of oblivion. The age of the epic was truly over in this world, and it was only by the purest chance that they had had the opportunity of glimpsing its last flickering before it was extinguished for good. They had captured the final glow and then lost it. The veil of night had fallen forever over the epic land.

Yes, that was it: night had fallen forevermore. For although they could not quite admit it to themselves, they could imagine a second visit only as an excursion into an icy sphere whence life had departed, where it would hardly be possible to make out in the dust the marks of the white stick of the Great Bard whose riddle they had sought to solve.

Such were the musings of Bill and Max as their dray

took them back to the town of N——, where they were to stay until the end of the week, when the bus would come to take them to the capital.

Unlike their last stay, they did not venture out of the hotel and met no one. The last locals with whom they had any dealings were the manager of the Globe Hotel and Blackie the porter, who lugged their suitcases to the bus station, then hobbled over to the bar, where, for reasons unknown, he drank himself silly and started talking about his first wife, whom no one had ever heard of before.

Some time passed. It was the middle of a perfectly ordinary week for the little town, a week devoid of any event whatsoever, with an amount of drizzle exceeding the climatic norm for the season and the place. But the excess of light rain suited the town all the same; it was in harmony not just with its architecture but also in a sense with its whole way of life. The monotonous patter seemed to be an attempt to help people bear the burdens that weighed them down, to alleviate their fate of being at the margin of real life.

The last winter had in fact brought them a whole series of exceptional events, though it had all begun slowly and almost imperceptibly. The arrival of the foreign scholars, the link that had been established once and for all between this place and Homer, the gossip and fantasies of the women, the enigma of the Buffalo Inn, then the arrival of the English-speaking spy, the mysterious attack on the inn, the bloody chains, the horde of journalists from Tirana — these events were more than a backwater like N—— could bear, especially as they all took place in a single season.

Now it was all fading away. In the cafés, the skeptics who had at the start been against all that imaginative nonsense and had then given in to collective pressure were now holding forth with conviction: "It's our own fault, you know. We didn't need to link the name of our town with a fellow who died four or five thousand years ago! For sheer stupidity, that takes the cake! If it had all been about opening a ketchup factory or the spa people have been going on about for ages, there might have been something to say for the fuss, but that Homeric business was just nonsense! Romantic nationalism, that's what it is! Outdated fetishism! You might as well try to put a halter on a ghost! And what kind of a ghost, I ask you — a blind ghost!"

The café audiences nodded wisely, as if to say: Yes indeed, how could we have been so stupid as not to think of all that? Good grief, a blind ghost! Well, thank goodness the whole business is over now, without any more harm done, because it could all have turned out much worse.

That is what the barflies thought, but the opinion of the town's gynecologist that Thursday afternoon was rather different. He was standing at the large bay window on the first floor of his house, part of which had been converted into a private clinic, and was watching the young woman whom he had just examined walking down the narrow alley in the rain, stepping carefully so as to avoid the puddles.

On the doctor's elongated face, somewhere between

the chin and the lower lip (because of its curious shape, the doctor's face differed from a normal physiognomy in all its proportions) there hovered something like a smile, expressing either a mildly ironical anxiety or the pleasure of having a morbid curiosity finally satisfied after years of waiting.

No, it wasn't all that easy to remove all the consequences of the two foreigners' visit to N——.

His eyes swept over the coldly glinting medical instruments lined up on the white-painted shelves. No, to make all the consequences disappear from that woman, for instance, he was going to have to use certain of those instruments on her.

"Incredible!" he exclaimed, as he looked down once more at the alleyway, where she was no more to be seen. He had been waiting so long for the day when she would come for treatment at his clinic! Season followed upon season, and still she did not come. "It seems she'll never deceive her governor!"

But now she had come, just as he had stopped believing that she would ever need his services. As he had expected, she was pregnant.

She had sat with flushed cheeks as he pronounced his verdict: "Madam, you are pregnant." Without waiting for him to ask her to explain anything, as if they had enjoyed a tacit understanding for years, she had begun to talk. No, she wouldn't hide it from him, there was no point in any case, she would hide nothing from him, she had had an adventure with one of the two learned scholars, more precisely with the one who had glaucoma. . . . That was what she had said, in an almost mechanical prattle, as if she had learned it by heart, while she hurriedly put her clothes back on, her eyes fixed firmly on the exit door, and she hadn't answered his question about the date on which she could have the operation, nor did she respond to his final words of assurance that even though he was only a country doctor he was a gentleman nonetheless and that she could trust that her husband would never know anything at all. . . .

Well, well, well . . . , the doctor mused, still standing at the window, made opaque by the rain. Who could guess what really goes on in the back of beyond? And he felt a pang of regret, like a bout of rheumatism brought on by the damp, that he had never made a record of all the bizarre episodes that had cropped up in the course of his long career.

It must have been the same day that Bill Norton and Max Ross, wrapped in traveling capes, stood on the deck of the Durres–Bari steamer and watched the coast of Albania recede into the distance. Actually, only Max was watching, because Bill could not really see anything anymore. During the week they had spent waiting for the ferry, Max had tried to persuade his companion to resume the eye drop treatment, but Bill received these pleas with profound indifference. Once, he said he would start proper treatment when he got back to New York, but his tone made his fatalistic attitude pretty clear.

Max looked at his friend from the side and recalled that he too had once felt resigned to a disastrous end. Homer's revenge . . . He tried in vain to rid himself of

that thought, but it had wormed its way into his mind.
Perhaps that was how the Blind Bard would always take
his revenge on those who sought to solve his riddle . . . ?

The mere thought made Max shudder. Was the loss
of sight perhaps a necessary precondition for entering the
Homeric night?

He shook himself as if to cast off these gloomy musings. Remembering that he had bought the day's newspaper on the dockside and still had it in his pocket, he
took it out and, struggling to prevent the wind from
blowing the paper away, said to Bill:

"Hey, look! We're in the news. . . ."

"Really?"

They found a wind-sheltered spot, and Max read the
article to himself first of all.

"The trial of the bandits will start very soon," he
said to Bill a few minutes later in the midst of his reading. "There's an interesting hypothesis about the instiga-
tors. . . ."

"Really?"

"They're saying something about Serbs," said Max
as he tried to flatten down the wind-blown newspaper.

"Do you remember that monk with the jolly face?"
Bill remarked.

The paper in Max's hands flapped about dement-
edly.

"Listen to what it says here, though: 'This is not
the first time that Slav chauvinists have brutally attacked
scholars working on Albania's classical roots. Any mention of the Illyrian origins of the Albanians, in particu-

lar, arouses in them barbaric and murderous jealousy, which is, alas, just as widespread here, in the Balkans.' Well . . . hang on, what's this? 'Anyone who deals directly or indirectly with this topic is in their eyes an enemy. And the hand that wielded the crowbar that struck down the Yugoslav scholar Milan Sufflay in a Zagreb back street some ten years ago did not tremble at the prospect of slaying two Homeric researchers from across the Atlantic.'"

Bill touched the place on his head where he had been hit. He could still feel the swelling.

"But look here, there's something else about us on the inside pages."

Max's brow furrowed impatiently as he read on. He nodded once or twice, seemed about to smile, then muttered: "Unbelievable!"

"So what is it?" Bill asked.

"It's incredible, Bill!" said Max, without raising his eyes from the paper. "The *epivent* we were waiting for . . . well, here it is! And do you know what the subject is? It's the most recent episode you could possibly imagine: it's an epic poem . . . about us!"

"What are you saying?"

"Look here. Oh, but of course you can't make out the letters. . . . Sorry, Bill, I got carried away. Wait, I'll read it aloud. 'A black *aprath* rose from the waves. . . .' That's how it begins."

"What? What do you mean?" Bill stammered.

"'A black *aprath* rose from the waves. . . .' "

"What's an *aprath*? I don't get it."

199

"I suppose it's an Albanian version of the German word *Apparat,* meaning a piece of equipment — that's the tape recorder," said Max. "Yes, it has to be that. Hey, listen to the rest of it:

> "*A black* aprath *rose from the waves.*
> *Some said it came for our good.*
> *It will bring only grief, said the others.*
> *Some said it brings frozen nightingales to*
> *life.*
> *By God, it freezes the* lahuta, *said the*
> *others. . . .*"

Max looked up as if to share his friend's astonishment. He could not yet believe what he had read.
"Is there more?" Bill asked. "Go on!"
Max swallowed and continued to recite from the page:

> "*Hermit Frok came out of the cave*
> *Where he had been hiding for seven years*
> *Some think him a good man —*
> *He is evil incarnate, say the others.*
> *O Lord! He lay into the* aprath,
> *He made it bleed black bile —*
> *Slowly pulled out all its entrails,*
> *And the hills and the heavens shook with*
> *his cries. . . .*"

Max glanced up at his friend once again. Bill had recently acquired a kind of detached stare that seemed quite impenetrable.

"It really is about us . . . ," he said reflexively in Albanian.

"What a tragic misunderstanding!"

It was too late now to try to put it right. By the fact of that misunderstanding, they had now become an integral part of a mysterious universe. Things had come full circle.

There was a long blast on the ship's horn. Max was about to go back to reading the paper, but the expression forming on Bill's face suddenly held his attention. It was as if something were about to boil over on that inwardly thunderstruck face, with its aging, windburned, leathery skin, its eyes, like those of the more or less completely blind, seemingly made of stone.

"A black *aprath* rose from the waves . . . ," Bill mumbled.

Somewhat taken aback, Max was on the point of asking, "What do you mean?" but he realized that the question itself would have no meaning.

Suddenly, with a gesture that seemed to belong to another body, Bill pulled his right arm from under his cape, raised it to his face, splayed his fingers, placed his palm against his upper cheek and ear so that his fingers made a kind of ridge visible over the top of his head. *Majekrah*, Max thought, but he had no time to ponder it, because his companion had meanwhile begun to chant, in a flat and expressionless voice, the lines of verse that he had just heard read to him.

He repeated them with amazing accuracy, and the monotonous tune of his chanting enhanced their distance, making them seem to come from far away in time and space.

Good God! thought Max. He really is ill. He's going to die. . . .

The word *death* crossed his mind twice over, but strangely it now seemed devoid of any significance. It was only a shell that encased something else.